CW00406239

CAT KNIGHT

The Haunting of Murat Mansion

CAT KNIGHT

Disclaimer

This story is a work of fiction, any resemblance to people is purely coincidence. All places, names, events, businesses, etc. are used in a fictional manner. All characters are from the imagination of the author.

Table of Contents

Chapter One

From the moment she saw it, she knew.

Ruby Murat stared up at the house. Specifically, at the topmost window. That round window, resting in the downturned V shape formed by the roof, like the solitary eye of a cyclops. An eye that she could see, even from here, had been robbed of its usual function by a thick layer of black paint. Paint applied, from inside. Paint applied, so Charles Winsome had said, because in Mr Murat's attic there was no need of a window. It was a place that only looked in'. Charles Winsome had said the attic was the focal point. The place where the darkness dwelt and seeped inwards. He referred to it as room of darkness and sorrow, yet even then, it was a room that was rumoured to hold immense financial worth.

But somehow Ruby knew. She could feel it, even then, watching, surveying. This house didn't just 'look in'. This house, knew she was there. It knew who she was. This house, had been expecting her.

The building itself was immense. A stone-built edifice, it stood, monolithic in its isolation, like a great black tombstone upon the heath.

It's only companion, was a huge, leafless elm, the gnarled, ancient branches which writhed upwards like swirls of ink dropped into water, grazing the building's left side and giving it the appearance of a prop or walking stick, supporting the house's weathered old bones. Ruby hated it, but still, she'd had to come.

The letter had arrived with the autumn. It had drifted, like the russet leaves from the trees, noiselessly down from the letterbox and onto the welcome mat where it nestled quietly, waiting to be found.

Yawning and thinking of other things Ruby Murat had lifted the letter and placing it on top of the other brown envelopes (bills, she'd thought ominously) had padded barefoot toward her favourite nook to read them.

This was her routine, and this was her spot. At least for now she'd thought. The 'nook' as she called it was a window seat. The cushioned ledge protruding out a few feet to allow you to curl, back resting against a pillow, beside the window that framed the garden like a painting. From the first day she had loved it. Sitting, knees raised with a steaming cup of good coffee close to hand, she would come here every morning and watch as the golden light streamed, fresh and bright through the airy expanse of the kitchen. Here, before Pete ever woke, she would enjoy an hour. Reading the paper, her book or the mail. The day the letter came she had rested back with a sigh. Better enjoy it whilst it lasts, she thought. It will be gone soon.

They had married in the spring. Ruby glanced towards the wedding photo, now face down on the counter. She knew the image anyway. The time of year had suited their mood.

New, emergent and full of potential; those were the green shoots of their love. In the photo, the colour palate and Ruby's appearance was spring, her golden hair and the crisp white dress bathed in the joy of all that felt new. It was new then, she pondered.

For a while summer had been glorious, their new home perfect. Unfortunately, Summer had also been the name of Pete's other woman. The marriage was over before it started.

Spring had meant joy. Summer had brought pain, autumn, she knew was a long march to loss. Her husband, this house, her home. All would be gone by winter.

Looking now at the garden, laid with a carpet of orange brown leaves, beautiful but soon to be mulch, she felt for a moment the same sense of decline. Autumn had arrived. She lifted the brown envelopes with their uniform banality and pushed them aside in favour of the letter, robed in white. She looked again at the leaves and felt the cool of the outside pressing itself against the glass window, she sipped her coffee and sliding one finger beneath the fold, opened the letter. "Winter's not here yet," she thought.

***

It was still autumn the day she arrived at the house, though standing before it, the wind's icy chill biting through her coat, it felt unquestionably like winter. Though it was morning, the moon was still visible in the sky, as if reluctant to let the night pass. She had arrived in Scotland by train that morning, her things waiting in storage and an appointment with the solicitor, based in Edinburgh, arranged for the following week.

It had taken a long drive and a short but icily cold ride in small fishing boat to reach the island, just off the Northern coast, where Charles and more importantly the house had been waiting.

Ruby read and reread the first paragraph of the letter. It was handwritten, something which struck her as unusual in this era of computers and emails. She couldn't remember the last time she had seen, let alone received a handwritten letter. Even Pete's card to her on her wedding day had been printed. The message entered into a textbox on some website that printed cards.

This missive was like a relic, the calligraphy, a beautiful flowing hand made her wonder whether she could incorporate the image somehow into her work. When Ruby had read the name of the sender 'Charles Winsome Art Dealer,' —she had immediately hoped that her work would be the subject of the letter. Frames, canvases, clays, paints and pencils were propped against every available surface and she could not help but hope that Charles Winsome might represent a gallery or collector looking to purchase some of her creations. But alas, no. This letter was not about her work, this letter, was about something else entirely.

"Dear Ms Murat"

it began, creating in just three words a fresh sting of hurt. She would indeed be forced to return to 'Ms', that deliberately ambiguous title she had favoured before her wedding. Neither an unmarried 'Miss' or the labelled 'Mrs' her mother had always taught her was somehow subservient. Neither owned, nor alone, just 'Ms'. She sighed deeply.

She had embraced Mrs with 'Luton' her married name, but the divorce would return her to her maiden name and to the title 'Ms', a return which despite all of her feminist values, felt like a demotion. The letter went on.

"I hope you'll excuse my writing to you unsolicited, but I felt it would be prudent of me to contact you and appraise you of your new situation. My name is Charles Winsome. Within the next few days—if you have not already—you will receive a letter from a solicitor concerning the estate of my client Auguste Murat. Your great uncle."

Ruby had raised her eyebrows at this, despite there being no one but her cat Rodger around to see the expression. As far as she knew, she didn't have a great uncle. She didn't even have an uncle. Her only living relative whom she was aware of was her mother who lived many thousands of miles away in Australia and to whom she hadn't spoken to in years.

"Whilst no doubt this letter will inform you of the material wealth you are likely to inherit in terms of bricks and mortar. I felt it necessary to make you aware of the far greater inheritance you will have been bequeathed upon receipt of the house. I can assure you, even at this stage and without entering the property, that it extends to many times the value of the structure itself..."

Before finishing the letter she rifled through the brown envelopes she had pushed aside. One, substantially thicker than the rest and too heavy to be a bill presented itself immediately and she hurriedly tore the flap. The letter head made her heart skip. It bore the name of a solicitor.

It took her ten minutes to finish reading and re-reading the letters, a further two hours to research details mentioned and another one hour to make her decision.

By midday she'd decided, this house, this window seat, this marriage and this life all would be consigned to the past. It's easier to accept your missteps she mused when the path ahead becomes clear. Throughout their relationship and brief marriage Pete had harboured secrets. Now it was her turn. Let him wait she thought. Scooping Rodger up into her arms she stood for a moment before her window and her nook pausing to bow a silent goodbye. Then she went upstairs and over the next three hours packed the belongings and materials she would need. By the time the autumn sun had set that day Ruby Murat was on a train heading north. She didn't leave a note.

Nor she knew, was she the only one keeping secrets.

Winsome's letter, exciting as it was, provided little in the way of clarity. It hinted and suggested, offering glimpses of its treasure but never with explicit description. Partly, Ruby realised, because Winsome himself didn't know. He had promised that the contents of the house would be valuable and had described in the most general of terms the nature of those contents but even then, much was conjecture and guess work.

Still, he had been right about the solicitor's letter, what reason did she have not to trust him? Plus, she had to admit, there was something romantic and adventurous about the mystery of it all. It was intriguing, especially the part about the attic.

It would be wrong to suggest that she didn't have her doubts.

For her, the word 'attic' was one pregnant with negative connotations. Every time she read the phrase 'Black Attic' in Winsome 's fluid hand, she felt as if the words hung or sagged somehow within the line, possessing within their syllables some weight not present in the other words.

Yet, she reasoned, if Winsome's letter was to be believed, then what he had referred to as 'the Black Attic' in his letter, could truly be a positive thing, not to mention quite something to see.

"I hope you don't mind, but I did take the liberty of looking you up on the internet before contacting you." he had written. "I must say that your work is very impressive. Clearly the artistic gene runs in the family."

At first Ruby had been suspicious of this comment, faint praise in her experience, usually being a precursor to some request or demand. Clearly Winsome was 'buttering her up' for something.

'No', she thought. 'Don't do that. This is a good thing, be positive'. She took a deep breath and admonishing herself for always seeing the downside, (something she'd caught herself doing more often since finding out about Pete and Summer), she scolded herself out loud.

"Why so negative? Just accept the damn compliment and move on Ruby." Rodger, who had been snoozing by her feet, raised his head for a moment, clearly noting the angry tone and worried that he might inadvertently have been the culprit. Ruby scratched and nuzzled his head, confirming that he was not, and satisfied, went back to his busy schedule of lazing on a cushion. Ruby continued reading.

"As an artist yourself, perhaps you have heard of Goya"?

She certainly had. In fact, she had written her dissertation for a degree in Art History on the Spanish artist.

"Though many people don't know it, some of Goya's most striking and recognisable paintings, such as 'Saturn devouring his son' were not painted for commissions or even originally onto canvas."

Ruby instantly conjured up the image of Goya's painting. She knew it well and had even stood before it once, in the Muse del Prado in Madrid. In it, the giant Saturn - a crazed, wild eyed thing, with wiry, oversized limbs- grips the remains of a tiny human being. Looking directly at the viewer as if interrupted, but defiant, he brings the diminutive corpse to his gaping, cavernous mouth like a loaf of bread to be ripped asunder and rent apart.

The painting had always given Ruby the creeps reminding her as it did of the Lovecraft stories she'd read as a teenager, stories about immense, dark things that consume souls. Shapeless immensities that would, given the chance, take all that we have, all of human progress and understanding, and chew it, like a dog with a toy.

Winsome 's letter went on.

"In his later years, terrified of descending into madness, Goya bought a house and retreated from society, becoming somewhat of a hermit. It was discovered after his death, that in his despair and alone in the house, he had bled out his anguish and confusion in paint. Goya painted the collection now known as 'The Black Paintings' directly onto the walls of this house.

A wild collection of gruesome sights they were never intended for public display. Today, they are worth millions. I am pleased to tell you that within the small circle of collectors who truly appreciate your uncle's work, a single commissioned portrait can sell for upwards of £175,000."

Until that moment, Ruby had always believed the phrase 'jaw dropping' to be hyperbole for effect, reading that figure and for the first time in her life, she felt her mouth, either through shock or excitement, open involuntarily.

"Save for these paintings and his correspondence with me, your uncle has had no contact with the outside world for over twenty years. He has not been seen in public for nearer thirty and no one, not even I, his closest friend and confident have entered his home, a home where it has long been rumoured his greatest masterpieces reside. I cannot, within these few short lines convey to you the mythic, almost legendary status that Murat's Black Attic has amongst collectors, but if that room, that dark tabernacle of your uncle's genius, contains what we believe it to contain, it's value will be immeasurable."

Whilst she appreciated Winsome 's enthusiasm, Ruby felt sure that the value would in fact be measured, and then, hopefully, written onto a pleasingly large cheque.

Chapter Two

The first thing Ruby noticed about Charles Winsome upon arriving at the house was his hands. Clearly whomever had written the letter with the beautiful handwriting and indeed signed it at the bottom, it was not Charles Winsome. His hands, pale and discoloured hung limply before him as if they had been pinned to his wrists as an afterthought, the bones and sinews twisted together at such angles that for him the act of simply holding a pen would have been quite impossible.

Even beyond this detail, it couldn't be denied that Winsome was an odd-looking man. tall with straight thin lips and pinched, weasel like features, his protuberant eyes, which darted furtively around as he spoke gave him a sly, slightly feral appearance made worse by his disconcerting habit of looking past you as he was speaking, as if at all times he was searching for someone on the horizon, or waiting for someone else to join the conversation.

Despite his odd appearance, Winsome was as polite and courteous in real life as he was in writing. Though it was clear that he was having trouble disguising how eager he was to get into the house and particularly up to that attic room.

Indeed, when she had called to inform him that she was stopping briefly in the village to pick up some provisions, he had seemed agitated if not positively crestfallen at the prospect of having to wait a few more minutes and had urged her to hurry, even suggesting that perhaps she could go later, after they had been inside the house. Looking at the distance between the village and the house she didn't much fancy the idea of the lonely and no doubt rain sodden walk into town later that evening and reasoned instead that if she was to stay at the house as planned for the coming week at least, essentials like milk, bread and some fruit could be purchased on the way. Charles, she decided, like Pete, could wait.

And so, Charles waited. Whilst she picked up these items he simply stood, fidgeting madly in anticipation. Soon, soon, she would be here, and he would be able to enter. For now, as he had for the past week, he could only stand, a dark silhouette, hunched as if in reverence before the great house. To enter without her, to approach the throne empty handed, he knew, was unthinkable. Instead he must simply wait, wait and listen. Listen for the sound that lay beneath. Beneath the wind and the distant hiss and shush of the waves, beneath the strangled calls of the seabirds and the splash, listen intently for the faint but ever-present buzzing hum of flies.

***

Ruby had hardly had chance to open the door and place the groceries onto the living room table before Winsome suggested they ascend the stairs and explore the attic. Juggling the groceries, a heavy bag of personal items and Rodger's carry cage, it was far from being Ruby's top priority.

"Bloody hell Charles, let me get through the door will you"? She said, smiling in an attempt to soften the severity of the comment but being at least half serious. Winsome checked himself and sweeping an imaginary piece of lint from the front of his dark buttoned up suit, with one sadly disfigured hand he replied quietly.

"Of course," he said "I didn't mean to rush you. I'm just…" he hesitated, searching for the right word, "I'm just… enthusiastic." he finished weakly, offering an apologetic smile, that, almost childlike, softened his features a little. Ruby placed the items on a large wooden table and laughed. Her plan, which she had shared with Winsome over the phone, was to use the house as a form of retreat, embracing the isolation of the place and taking the opportunity to get some time for work and importantly, some distance.

"I know. It means a lot to you, but if I'm going to actually *live* here, I need to sort a few things out first, you know?" she laughed.

"Of course." Winsome repeated maintaining his smile.

The interior of the house was stunning and somehow larger than it appeared from the outside. The wooden staircase that Winsome was so keen to climb stood directly opposite the front door across a large parlour or reception area, in the centre of which a small table upon which a vase filled with long dead flowers stood. To the left of these stairs was the living room into which Ruby had stumbled with her groceries, to the right, the kitchen and dining room.

Though she would have referred to it as the living room, the room in which the pair now stood was in many ways more like a study. The walls on two sides being lined from floor to ceiling with shelves, all of which were crammed to bursting point with old and clearly well-thumbed volumes. Many of these books were evidently old and had titles written in languages that Ruby didn't recognise.

By the door was a solid looking mahogany table that Ruby felt somewhat guilty about bundling her shopping onto it, the fresh food seeming somehow out of place and jarringly anachronistic, like a neon sign in an exhibit of antiquities. Ruby placed her hands on her hips and turning slowly surveyed the room curiously.

In time, her eyes fell upon the portrait. Her blood ran cold.

For an instant, Ruby felt as if she had fallen headlong into a colourless void. An airless vacuum where sound and breath did not exist. She would have found it hard to explain, but it was as if, with a single glance, it had somehow silenced the world. The gulls, which up until that point had shrieked and wheeled in the distance suddenly fell dumb, the wind, which had whistled against the angles of the house, hushed and halted as if its voice had caught in its throat. Though her companion was but steps away, for a moment, Ruby Murat knew she was alone with that portrait, with that image of him, of him and his shadow.

Suddenly the silence was broken. "That" Winsome said, noticing Ruby's fascinated gaze "is your great uncle, Auguste Murat."

"That," she replied, "is hideous." There was no doubt that the image was perfectly rendered.

Clearly her great Uncle was a man of extraordinary talents. The portrait, which hung above a large stone fireplace and had been done in oils had an almost photographic quality to it. And yet, for all the obvious talent, the undeniable skill and attention to detail displayed in the painting, there was something about it that was uniquely repulsive.

In appearance Auguste Murat resembled illustrations Ruby had seen by Dore of the fairy-tale villain Bluebeard, though in this portrait, his beard was far from blue, as far from blue and indeed from any colour as it was possible to be. Murat's beard was of an empty, incomparable black. A black so deep, so seemingly bottomless, that to view it was to despair at the sheer empty hopelessness of its tone.

It sat below his wild, staring eyes like the shadow of a shadow. So lifelike was the depiction that had it not been for the obvious difference in scale, it might easily have been possible to believe that the man pictured were actually standing in the room. The man, Ruby thought, or the men.

For the more disturbing element of the picture, more disturbing even than the hollow emptiness of that black, was the figure's shadow.

This form, which shared the same proportions as Murat himself was painted in the same terrible un-colour as Murat's beard. It stood to his left, peering over the shoulder and was somehow perfect and yet wildly incorrect.

Not only did it appear to be detached from the figure, in a way that shadows should not, but it retained, despite its shape, a three-dimensional roundness that shadows shouldn't have.

As if, rather than truly being a shadow, it was a portrait of the same man after having been immersed in a thick black liquid, an oil of tar, that clung in a smooth viscous sheen to the skin. This impression was underlined by the fact that despite being a shadow, this horrific apparition, this dark mockery of a human shape, *looked* at the viewer and even from the depths of that pit like darkness, smiled.

For rather than being simply a uniform silhouette, this shadow had eyes. Two milky orbs of endless malevolence that hung like stars in the night sky above two rows of crooked, pearlescent teeth, twisted into a horrific grin which shone out of the composition like some gothic reimagining of Lewis Carol's Cheshire Cat.

Ruby felt a wave of nausea chew at her stomach from the inside and with an effort of will, pulled her own eyes away.

Coughing loudly and deliberately to fill the room with sound and turning her back on the thing, she glanced back at Winsome.

"I hope you can find a buyer for that one" she said between coughs and motioning over her shoulder at the painting. "I'll tell you now. That'll be the first thing to go." Winsome 's smile had evaporated, replaced instead by the more familiar straight lipped stare.

"Perhaps.." he began "we should explore upstairs?" Ruby felt her stomach drop and for a flickering moment, she wondered whether she had made a mistake in coming here.

Two days ago, in London, the sense of spontaneity, of adventure and of escape had been exciting.

Now, cold, tired and not a little unnerved, the outlook was not nearly as bright. Even her visit to buy groceries had been unsettling.

The small village was quaint enough and harboured enough runaways from the mainland to warrant a post office and a small general store. Against the perennial grey of the sky, the village, with its warm ochre glow had seemed like a beacon or lighthouse, a sanctuary against the harsh and threatening heath.

And the people seemed friendly enough. The woman in the general store, who filled the space behind the small wooden counter as if it had been built around her, identified herself as Mrs Neet. She was politely curious, chatty and genuinely interested in seeing Ruby's work, even going so far as to invite her over to 'pop o'er for a spot a tea' one afternoon.

Ruby had liked her instantly and if she been the only occupant of the store, Ruby may have left the store feeling more upbeat. But sitting in an armchair, which had for some reason been placed to the left of the entrance at a right angle to the counter, sat an old man, who Mrs Neet identified as her father in law. His position, Ruby presumed was chosen to give him the chance to speak to each customer as they paid for their goods, and to make sure there was no funny business whilst the clerk's back was turned. But it was his choice of conversation unnerved her.

"You're off to Murat's old house eh?" he asked, almost furtively. "My ma used to say she'd tan our backsides if we ever went up there."

"Pipe down Da'. Ruby does'ne need to hear about your backside."

"I'm just sayin," Mrs Neet's father in law went on, "you watch yourself, there's an *Ogey* lives up in that house, up the attic they'd say." He smiled, a gummy, toothless grin "Don't you go messin about up there my ma would say, or that old Ogey man will get you." He dragged out the "oo" sound in the phrase 'old Bogey; so that it stretched and elongated, taking on an almost sing song rhythm as it was pronounced.

"Old Ogey?" Ruby had asked in disbelief.

"Aye" said the old man, staring directly at her now and shaking his finger in admonishment. Ruby picked up her things and moved to the door, never taking her eyes from the old man. She held the items tightly to her chest, as if to form a barrier.

"Pay no notice to him lovie. He's daft as a brush."

With an effort of will, Ruby again forced a smile and thanked them as Mrs Neet's father in law laughed, and, to a jarring, discordant melody, sang what sounded like an old nursery rhyme "*Old Bogey hums in the movin' black. To take you away in his big black sack.*"

So, Ruby had stepped out of the store and into the rain with the words of the rhyme sticking to hair and clothes like smoke, and it had followed her back to Auguste Murat's house. On most days she'd have laughed it off and regarded the old ghost story as actually quite quaint. She'd have laughed it off today too, had he not said, *Ogey,* because she had recognised the name as the one her own grandmother had scared her half to death with, telling her stories and warning her not to go to the attic because *'our Ogey'* would get her.

Now, here with the company of this strange man Charles Winsome, and with this disturbing portrait of her great Uncle, her composure was a thin veil hidden only by Ruby resting quietly in the sitting room, checking her phone messages. But the rhyme that had lisped from the rubbery mouth of that drooling old man, echoed in her head and between the portrait and the rhyme and the drooling old man, Ruby felt decidedly sick. Something—some intuition— playing at the corners of her mind warned her to run.

Bending down, she unhooked the door of the carry cage and let Rodger out. She watched as he took a few reticent steps, then ran back into the quilted shelter of the cage. She sighed deeply. *I know how you feel Rodge*. Perhaps, she thought, it had been a mistake. Perhaps, she should have stayed in London,

But this was to be her home now and no painting or creepy rhyme was turning her around. She gave the cat cage a gentle kick and, reluctantly, Rodger emerged, sniffing the air and calling loudly. Ruby closed the door of the cage. "No escape now Rodge."

Returning to standing, she turned to Winsome, set her jaw and spoke. "Let's explore upstairs." She said.

Chapter Three

The brief glimpse she caught of her bedroom was encouraging. It was large, contained an elaborate four poster bed and had sizeable windows on two sides. One even had a window seat. Ruby smiled to herself. This was better.

Her musings were only momentary however as Charles' enthusiasm once again got the better of him and he began almost immediately to ascend the second set of stairs. This time however, Ruby was happy to be swept along with the current. She had to admit that she too was curious about the attic's content and specifically it's value.

"Your room is unadulterated." Said Charles without turning around. "Auguste never used it. He slept up here."

"Unadulterated? You'll never make it as an estate agent Charles," she attempted to joke, mocking playfully the strange choice of adjective. Winsome did not respond and she reflected that the word, with all its connotations of pollution and corruption was probably not chosen by accident.

She watched as Winsome 's slender frame scurried up the stairs, seemingly struggling to fit his wide shoulders into the space, realising as she watched that the space was becoming narrower. Looking behind her she could see that each stair underfoot was slightly wider than one above.

The effect on perspective, aided by lines that had been painted on the walls in red and gold was dizzying, making the bottom of the stairs seem like a huge vista, which through these visual tricks, seemed increasingly further and further away.

Reaching the top stair, Winsome stopped dead. "Wait." He said fishing in his pocket, presumably for a key.

Ruby looked up at the door. The narrowness of the corridor made it seem somehow taller and more slender than it should be. It was of a heavy dark wood, painted, predictably, black. In the door's central panel was a small but beautifully ornate crown. It appeared to have been painted in gold leaf and against its dun background, it sparkled radiantly.

Winsome, who was clearly struggling, turned to Ruby, thrusting forward his right hip so that the pocket of his jacket was exposed to her. He held up his damaged hands in an apologetic gesture.

"Would you mind? It's somewhat difficult for me to get at."

"Of course," Ruby replied hastily, fishing in the pocket until her hands rested on the cold metal of the key.

She took it out and held it up for Winsome to see. He nodded, his breathing short and quick. Despite the chill in the house, a film of sweat had appeared on his forehead and upper lip, though not, she reflected, from the exertion of the climb.

Winsome was nervous. She gestured toward the lock, asking silently whether she should be the one to open it. Winsome pushed his two stumps together in a begging motion.

"Please, please do." With some difficulty he stood to one side to her allow her to squeeze into the space and push the key into the lock. It rattled into place with a satisfying click.

As it turned, she could feel Winsome 's breath, like the panting of a dog against her neck. The narrowness of the final step had pushed them uncomfortably close to one another and forced Winsome one step lower, but rather than taking a step back, on to the stair below that, he remained, like an obstruction blocking her exit, slowly but surely urging her forward.

Then the panting stopped. It was as if Winsome were holding his breath and again, the silence, the same awful silence that had blanketed the world when she looked at the portrait of Auguste Murat, fell upon the house.

She felt herself becoming nervous as she thought again of the portrait and more chillingly, of the shadow. "Old Bogey hums in the moving black," she thought.

Slowly, she turned the key, and with every incremental degree of rotation felt the oppressive presence behind her, the push and proximity, the weight in space of another body encroaching, closing and minimising the space. Shrugging her shoulder to accommodate, Ruby felt the space tightening and constricting ever smaller, her breath quickening as she leaned closer to the door, with each inch closer, the space behind closed until finally, she turned, knocking into and almost unbalancing Charles.

"Steady on Charles. It's a bit claustrophobic, do you want to give me some space? I think the door opens outwards." Winsome stared at her. Wide eyed, as if, he too thought, that he was being pushed, pressed from behind toward the door. There was a long pause.

"Oh...of course" he stuttered and, with what seemed like a great effort stepped backwards and down a few of the steps.

Ruby turned the handle with a wrenching jolt. Indeed, the door did open outwards and it was necessary for both Ruby and Charles to descend a few of the stairs to allow it to slowly yawn open.

As it did, Ruby felt her curiosity override her fear and shifting to one side, peered cautiously inside.

Or at least she would have, but to peer inside, however, was not an option. For behind the attic door extending purposefully from floor to ceiling was a great black wall. A solid partition of rough-hewn brick painted entirely black.

Despite the uniform colour the outline of each individual brick could be clearly made out. It occurred to Ruby almost immediately that at the edges, where this wall met the door's heavy frame only half or quarter bricks were visible. The wall it seemed extended past the parameters of the frame. Either the door and the wall in which it sat had been built around this black wall, or, far more likely, the wall had been erected from the inside.

This of course begged the question of how the wall's builder, having presumably bricked up the room's only exit would have escaped afterwards, but Ruby was not given time to ponder this conundrum.

Charles, having seemingly abandoned or forgotten all pretence of being patient or polite, virtually shoved her aside to reach the wall. Upon seeing it, a seemingly involuntary sound, like a whimper, escaped from somewhere deep in his chest. It was less disbelief than anguish.

His eyes in a panicked frenzy moved over the surface in horror, as his crippled hands traced impotently over the brickwork, as if he were searching for a key or weak point that would yield to pressure.

Suddenly, with an agonised shriek, Winsome began to pound and beat desperately against the wall as if hoping that somehow, he could, with only his fists force it into collapse.

Ruby looked on as Winsome 's senseless whimpering coagulated into something resembling words, a low guttural mantra that he repeated over and over as he beat, with reckless unrestrained force at the wall, the twisted knuckles and bony ridges of his wrists slamming with a wet slap into the unrelenting stone, until they came back torn and bloodied.

For a moment she was frozen in place, unsure both of what she was seeing and what she could do about it. After a second however, she came to her senses and, screaming for him to stop, lunged forward, trying with both hands to stop his desperate thrashing.

Her first thought upon trying to grasp his wrists was how surprisingly strong Winsome was, her second thought, was the momentary fear that in the struggle they might both tumble down the narrow stairs.

Luckily, her touch, her hands as solid tangible reminders of the concrete world outside of his hysteria seemed to stun Winsome back into some awareness of his surroundings.

The pounding stopped and with what seemed like an immense effort of will, he tore his gaze from the wall. Slowly and without a word she released her grip on Charles wrists. He immediately drew back his hands and like a mucky child swiping jam across pudgy cheeks, he streaked a smear of red brown blood onto his face as he tried in vain to wipe the tears from his eyes. Ruby guided him back down the stairs. It was only after they had reached the bottom stair opposite the front door that Winsome hesitantly spoke.

"I must apologise," he began sheepishly. "It must have been quite distressing for you to see that. It's just—" He paused, placing his battered hands behind his back out if sight. "— it's just, it can be very frustrating when you wait so long for something and then..." He was as usual looking past Ruby as he spoke, on this occasion into the living room and perhaps, she thought, at that awful portrait. "...and then well, *something* frustrates the process."

Winsome refused her offer of a towel for the wounds on his hands and pushing himself back up to his full height, his hands placed on the small of his back, attempted to go on as if nothing had happened. "As I'm sure you are aware, I am quite eager to see the contents of your Uncle's attic."

"Yeah, no shit" thought Ruby to herself, looking at the streaks of blood that still stained Winsome 's cheeks and which, though they were hardly visible against the black brickwork also adorned the wall of the Black Attic.

"Well, it'll come soon enough," she offered, before trying to reassure him that she could have the wall taken down, even going so far as to suggest that she could do it herself with a sledgehammer. This seemed to edge Winsome back toward panic.

"For heaven's sake, no!" He protested, "We have no way of knowing what might be on the other side of that wall! Tearing it down could destroy a masterpiece." He went on to vaguely explain a process by which part of the roof to that room could be removed in the coming days.

She had half a mind to protest his nonchalance at destroying part of what was, after all, her house now, but she let it pass. She doubted the roof was intact anyway, how else could the wall builder have escaped the room afterwards? Winsome made some garbled excuses, promising to return the next day and with a nod of the head left her alone.

Closing the door behind him she considered his words. Though she tried to stop it, her mind, kept returning, time and again, to a single turn of phrase. It was something he'd said. Some thing. Winsome hadn't blamed 'somebody' or 'someone' for 'frustrating the process.' Winsome had blamed *'something'*.

Still at least he'd finally gone and left her alone. She turned toward the living room. The house was achingly still and yet, somehow, not empty. It was as if the silence were itself a sheet of solid mass that filled the rooms, filling and expanding into every inch more than that though. The stillness seemed planned. It felt, somehow intentional.

Like a *thing* that lurks in anticipation, tendons flexed and taut in readiness, as a rubber band stretched to its fullest extent, perched on the cusp of reflex. The house, she thought, was waiting.

From somewhere upstairs the faint sound of a ticking clock seemed to stretch and swim through the silence. Someone or *something* she thought. Standing at the threshold to the living room. Ruby glanced fleetingly at the portrait and knew, as surely as she knew her own name, that although Charles Winsome had left, she was far from alone.

Rodger confirmed this, nuzzling playfully against her shin. Ruby sighed deeply and bent down to lift him.

"Well, this is home now Rodge. Guess we'd better get ourselves something to eat huh?" as she spoke, she was conscious of doing so in a deliberate overly loud manner, as if she were announcing her intentions as much to the house as to Rodger. "Yep," She confirmed out loud, "this is home and we're going to make the best of it." Her voice as she spoke sounded thin and unconvincing as if she'd tried with some blunt tool to slice through the silence only for it to bend and warp, never breaking, never pierced. Again, she sighed, steadying herself and paced into the living room.

Chapter Four

The first thing that struck her upon entering the room was the smell. Had it been there earlier? If so, why hadn't she noticed it? It was a base, sour odour. As she moved toward the table the stench became overpowering, it stabbed at the senses with a tart acidic potency, as if it were somehow possible to breath in stinging nettles.

Ruby covered her nose and mouth and looking towards the table saw the mass of putrid mulch that had earlier been her groceries. The whole lot, bread, meat, potatoes and fruit had rotted and putrefied, filling the bag with a thick brown juice that leaked over the table and dripped viscously onto the floor.

The meat, chicken, which only an hour ago had been perfectly fresh, writhed and squirmed with maggots, their plump white bodies the colour of yoghurt, sliding slickly and noiselessly over one another. Ruby gagged and retreated from the room.

How was it possible? Had the food been rotten when she bought it? To be fair, she hadn't seen a refrigerator in the shop, and she had been distracted by the old man's mutterings.

For a moment she wondered if that was a ploy, distract the customer, whilst Mrs Neet sold them the tainted goods. She dismissed the thought at once.

She had seen the food, held its comforting firmness in her hands. She would have noticed if it had been rotten, the food in that room was virtually liquified. Ruby thought back to the project she had done in her first year of art school, sketching a bowl of fruit on successive days as it decomposed. The piece had been inspired by a Carravagio painting she had seen in which, rather than the usual ripe bloom of swollen fruit, the artist had chosen to show some of the fruit past its best, tainted by the first thin shadows of decay.

Her pieces, first in pencil then in oils, using a sickly palette of off ripe colours, had been beautiful studies but had necessarily taken weeks. Not because she was slow to paint, or overly fastidious in the capturing of detail, but because she was painting from life, life and its slow descent into death, a slow descent which took time.

It should have taken weeks, even months for food to completely rot like that. Yet, though it should have been impossible she considered possibilities. The temperature of the room? The position on the table, some contaminant in the wood? Perhaps, she thought, there was some mould or mildew in the room, some damp or bacteria that, affecting the food through touch, had accelerated the process and caused it to rot. She considered these possibilities. Perhaps, they were possible.

Standing in the hallway she watched as Rodger scurried into the kitchen. She wiped her mouth, the nausea fading the further she ventured from the stench and called to him across the hall.

"Good idea Rodge." She said aloud, striding into the kitchen leaving the food and the impossible possibilities behind her.

Two hours later, seated at the kitchen's yellow pine table, she almost felt like herself. Though it made for a meagre repast, the bag of cashews nuts she had bought for the train but never eaten, filled her enough to stave off the hunger.

Now, sitting with a cup of steaming hot tea and the remains of a Twix, she allowed the warm coating sweetness of the chocolate to mix with tea and for a moment, almost smiled.

The kitchen itself was huge, the table at which she sat, was placed at a right angle to a stone-built breakfast bar, behind which was a stove and an L shaped expanse of worktops and cupboards.

For a moment she had considered making the journey back to Mrs Neet's to repurchase the items she had lost, but quickly decided against it, considering how odd it would look it she waltzed in like a Deja vu and bought the same list of items a second time.

It wasn't as if she could buy them discreetly either, the shop's 'counter and request' set up would make sure of that. Worse still, she might be called upon to explain why she was rebuying items she'd bought earlier that day and would be forced to come up with some clumsy excuse.

After all, she couldn't very well tell the truth, could she? That would sound mad and, in the telling, would force her to acknowledge to somebody else, the impossible things she was starting to imagine.

She took a long slurp of her tea, its familiar taste and satisfying warmth calming her a little and taking out her phone, began, with curiosity that skirted dangerously close to that of the fabled feline, to enter her searches into google. Her first search, for the name Auguste Murat, was fruitless. Clearly those who appreciated his work were careful to guard their interest. She pondered for a moment, as to how an artist with such little profile that he didn't even warrant a Wikipedia page, could be so sought after. But then, she reflected, perhaps that was the point.

She could definitely see how in that world of the so called 'art market', the idea of a talent being 'exclusive' could be a selling point. Why wouldn't those critics and toffee-nosed collectors love him? The notion of a 'known unknown' was perfect for their elitist pretensions.

An esoteric talent, secretly shared by only the most astute of aesthetes and circulated under clandestine conditions? Those idiots would lap it up. She thought for a moment of her own work and wondered if, when her things were delivered from the mainland the following morning, she would have time to paint in the evening. Back in London, she had loved to paint at night.

In the early hours, when the world slumbered, she felt, in the solitude, an energy almost like electricity. With a pot of strong coffee by her elbow and her iPod playing music that made her feel 'arty' she would pour her inspirations onto the canvas. The freedom of those hours felt, even in her memories, seemed a fluid, limber release and for a second she pined for her brushes.

She pictured herself in *this* house, raising her easel, and working in a fever of creativity, splashing on colour with liberal, almost balletic ease. Though perhaps, she thought, maybe not at night.

After wasting a few minutes revisiting the grand but wholly uninformative homepage of 'Winsome Fine Art Dealership' a site that yielded no more information on the third viewing than it had on the first two occasions she had visited it, she allowed her scope to widen. "Old Bogey hums in the moving black, to take you away in big black sack," she mouthed noiselessly as she typed in the words 'folklore' 'bogeyman' 'children' and 'sack'. A few minutes later, she wished that she hadn't.

To say that the stories themselves scared her would be inaccurate. The fables told to frighten children would hardly hold weight for a sceptical woman of twenty-nine, would they? Would they?

To start with, as she skimmed through the stories of monsters that took away children in sacks, Ruby remained unmoved. In her head, behind the words, she could almost hear her own calm voice. I am untouched, I am unscathed, it said as it proudly affirmed that these words, stories, tales for children, they, all of them, meant nothing.

Even after the events of the day, even in this creepy setting, the stories simply flowed over the surface of her mind, unable, despite all of their sinister content, to raise within her one iota of fear. Yet, as she continued to read however, she listened again for that voice, and heard with alarm, as that voice began to crack.

33

It wasn't one story that scared her, it was the 'more than one', it was 'the many'. The fact of the many. How could that be? Somehow across countries, continents and oceans the story was the same. A man or monster, someone or something, that took away children, 'in his big black sack' took them away to be tortured or eaten. Never to be seen again. The stories were just stories, but the ubiquity was a fact.

The more she read the more of the same she found. The story was everywhere. She read of Slovakia where they called it the Bubak, in Poland the Bubek, in Russia Bubay, differing names but always the same. In India Bori Baba, in Algeria Bouchaka, in Turkey Karqhyt, Goni Billa in Sri Lanka, the list went on.

From Hondurous and Mexico with El Robas Chicos 'The snatcher of Children' to Vietnam with Ong Ba Bi, Switzerland, South Africa, Armenia, Tunisia and, with a name that turned Ruby's stomach, in Haiti, where the thing was 'Uncle Gunnysack'. Wherever you went, it went. It was there, always there, in moving black, dark and behind. Like a shadow.

Ruby closed the search. She pushed away her chair with a loud scrape that made Rodger, who had been circled on the table itself jump to his feet and spring to the floor.

For a moment she simply stood. Then, with a deep exhalation, she pushed her open palms downward, dropping her shoulders in a 'hush now' gesture. For the umpteenth time that day, she spoke to herself out loud.

"Jeez Ruby, get a grip. They'll be taking you in a straight-jacket never mind a sack."

She sighed hard again, noticing as her heartbeat began to settle, just how quickly it had been beating.

****

In the bedroom, *her* bedroom, *Ruby* felt, for the first time that day as if she could relax. Winsone's choice of the word 'unadulterated' had seemed odd at the time, but now, sitting on the edge of the four-poster bed, she could appreciate the turn of phrase.

The room 'felt' different. The close, stifling stillness that seemed to fill the other rooms like a viscous liquid, was absent here. Here there was a woody almost cinnamon-like aroma and, owing to the fact that the window had been left open, the circulation of fresh, clean smelling air. The room itself, like all of the others in the house was large and ornately furnished. The bed was of a heavy mahogany with intricately carved bed posts that, Ruby reflected, must have cost a fortune and were probably of great age.

She lay back against the pillow. Despite having not been disturbed for many years, the bedclothes didn't seem stiff, but were instead, comfortable. She would however, banish them to a cupboard as soon as her own bedding arrived, along with her other things the following day.

The curtains of the four-poster bed were of a thick, luxuriously red velvet and tied back. Ruby considered leaving them that way but reflected that having them down would likely keep out the North Scottish chill, besides which, there was something richly appealing about the idea of being enclosed. As if, by drawing these heaven curtains she could create a sanctuary shut off from the rest of the house.

She listened to Rodger's quiet purring. He had clearly had a similar idea and hadn't felt like waiting for Ruby to agree before settling himself for the night by her side. She drew the heavy curtains and rested back laying on her side, still fully clothed, cushioned by the pillows, her mind hushed softly by the clock's lulling tick. Relaxed, slowly Ruby begin to drift, cocooned by that sweet veil of sleep. She did not turn off the light.

CRASH

Startled to waking by the thudding crash above her she wondered for a moment where she was. Naturally disoriented by her surroundings rubbing her eyes she sat bolt upright. A thin trickle of icy sweat inched down her spine. She listened. Her breath was heavy but around it, nothing but silence.

Or at least, near silence.

For beside her on the bed, his back arched in a terrible curve, limbs and sinews stiffened in readiness, Rodger wailed and hissed in a way she never before seen. As she came to her senses, her eyes rested on the end of the bed. On the thick velvet curtain at the foot of the bed where Rodger's eyes, improbably wide, were fixed. She paused, stock still and listened. Holding her breath, she, allowed her ears to grasp at the silence.

Ruby froze. Below, the sound of his mewling, faint but distinct, someone else was breathing.

Chapter Five

The curtain before her was far too thick to allow a shadow to fall from outside. Instead, it hung in insolent uniformity, a single wall of colour, concealing as much as it shielded. Ruby continued to hold her breath. Listening. It was there. Laboured, wheezing, as if the air were percolating, drawn into lungs half filled with soil. There, unmistakably was —breathing. Ruby's heart rose to her throat. If she kept as quiet and still as she could, perhaps somehow she would go unnoticed.

No, that was stupid. It knew she was there.

There was a pause, a moment that seemed, to extend, a chasm of hours. As she looked on in silent horror, the folds in the long fabric drapes slowly yawned forward. Two small points, like errant waves on the surface of an otherwise glassy sea, pushed inward toward her, as if someone, or something, were pressing their hands against it standing behind the curtain and pushing at its weight.

"Who's there?!" she screamed, drawing up her knees in fear that a hand, bone thin and muscular, might reach through that gap and clutch, with terrifying strength at her ankle.

She clenched her teeth tried with all of her might to smash and force her fear back into the shape of anger. She raised herself onto her hands and knees.

"Who the fuck is there!" she spat and conjuring more bravery than she ever thought she had, tore back the curtain, to fight or to run.

Instead, she fell.

Careering forward, she overbalanced, tumbling onto the floor at the edge of the bed. Rodger sprang like lightning to the floor and both looked up, in terror, at nothing.

One thick curtain. A curtain no doubt hung from this rail for decades, lay torn and crumpled on the floor. Behind it the empty space mocked her.

Nothing. Nothing was there.

But, she thought, scrabbling back and clutching her bruised shoulder, there had been something. At that same instant, she again heard the crash.

It came from above. As if someone were flinging an immense weight, a hammer or bowling ball against the floor of the room above, pounding and hammering as if to smash a rent in the ceiling and force their way through into this room.

Ruby remained fixed, her eyes glued to the spot above the bed. Between the thuds, each dull impact, there was a lighter, more familiar sound. A sound she recognised, as footsteps.

A break in? She thought and conjured images, laughable as they seemed, of a limber young man clambering up the tree, and somehow, for some reason, dropping through some unseen hole into the attic above.

Even as the image flashed before her eyes, she knew she didn't believe it. Ruby knew there was no young man up there in her Uncle's black, troubled attic.

"No." She heard herself say out loud. "Dead people are just that; dead. They don't get up for a midnight stroll or start moving furniture at 3am." Whatever or whoever was making that noise, it wasn't Auguste Murat. And it wasn't going to scare her from her own damn house.

Rising to her feet, she tried again, more successfully this time to channel her fear into anger. She felt the throbbing in her shoulder and pushed against it, tightening her fists into balls. The noise above continued. "Fuck you," she spat through her teeth as she marched for the door.

Moving barefoot across the landing, as if pushed physically from behind by her own knotted self-will, she turned the corner to that second flight of stairs and, staring up at the great black door, paused for a second and started to ascend.

As she walked, her heart pounding, the liquid in her mouth and throat seemingly stirred to a porridge like thickness. Gradually, her forward momentum slowed, as if fighting her way through syrup. As she moved, the narrowing steps and decreasing angle shaved her resolve away. The walls sliced, and sheared away at her shell, her skin, her flimsy film of will. With every step, Ruby felt torn down to a tiny, helpless core, and with it her rage had given way, to fear. The sounds had shrunk as well, lesser, but still present, reduced to slow shuffling thuds.

'There is someone in there' she thought. Someone or something. Ruby felt her confidence continue to shrink.

With the shrinking, it seemed as though she was aging backwards, to those days, when at six and half years old, the Bogey and the attic had stalked her in her dreams and fear gripped her soul.

"Get it together Ruby" she told herself aloud, "I might be scared, but I won't be scared away." She slowed to a halt as she approached the top stairs. It was only hours earlier that she had almost been pressed against the wood by Winsome 's greedy enthusiasm, to get entry to the room. It seemed a lifetime ago.

She paused, staring once again at the great black door and listened. There it was. There below the shuffling, a low but constant hum, as of some electrical fault. *Perhaps that explains it, just a fault in the wire.* All at once, the noises stopped. Again, silence reigned.

As if a step removed, seeing herself in a dream, Ruby watched helplessly as her hand, filmed and damp with perspiration, groped and extended toward the handle. Her heart beating wildly with its rushing thud sounding in her ears. All at once she realised that she wasn't breathing, but standing, taut and flexed like a fine steel wire. Slowly, quietly, she allowed herself to breath and with one smooth action, she opened the door.

The wall hard and impenetrable as it ever was, loomed before her. Lit now only by the furthermost strain of light from the room below, the wall seemed, impossibly, blacker than it had. And yet, across its coal-shade segments, she could still see the thick, brown clots of once red smears. Winsome 's blood, as he beat and bashed to be inside.

Avoiding these streaks, Ruby placed her hands, the outstretched palms, against the brick. Hard and cool beneath her touch it pushed stolidly back against her, as she brought her ear closer and closer to its surface, listening as best she could for movement within. Holding her weight in her hands, she leaned over the top stair and inch by inch allowed herself to crane her ear forward, to edge closer to the wall, hearing as she did, the remnants of sound, the whispering shuffle from inside. For a split second her ear glanced the brick, then, as gravity ripped the floor from beneath her, she fell, headlong, through it.

Ruby Murat hit the ground with a hard, wet slap, her forearms taking the brunt of the fall but not enough to prevent her head from slamming into the boards. She spun and reeled, flailing blindly away from the pain and thrusting for purchase, pushed herself up to a seated position, facing whence she'd come.

In disbelief she looked at the wall. Or where, she knew, a wall should have been. In its place, across the doorway, was a huge, torn canvas. An immense rent through its middle, marking the spot where she had fallen straight through its surface, ripping it in two and creating in the middle, a man-sized tear, a vertical slash through which the only light entered the room.

Chapter Six

On the back of the canvas, as no doubt, on the front, was painted, in photographic detail so clear it felt like a painted lie, the image of a black brick wall.

Tromp d'eoiil thought Ruby- 'trick of the eye'.

She had seen such paintings before. Oil work, intended to make the viewer believe that rather than an a 2D shape wrought in paint, there was in fact an object, solid and real. It took skill, but it was possible.

That her uncle, the painter behind the portrait downstairs could have painted such a thing she was in no doubt. He clearly had the requisite level of skill. He could have done it, but she knew, had seen and felt only moments ago, he hadn't. Ruby stomach roiled and churn as the hairs on her arms rose high.

It *had* been a wall. She had watched, as Charles Winsome, had slammed his mockeries of hands into that wall until they bled. It did not yield a single atom, and his flesh and bone torn from his pounding. *That was no canvas. That was a wall.*

It was in that moment, seated and staring at the glimpse of the stairs that was visible through the rip, Ruby felt as though she had been birthed into the room. She turned her head quietly, terror clawing at every nerve in body to look at her Uncle's Black Attic.

Relief flooded her. It was a space. That was all. Large, open and importantly, uninhabited. She was alone. Whoever or whatever made those noises, had bled back into the shadows of her imagination. As far as she could see, she was by herself, alone but for paintings.

Merciful God, the paintings.

Reaching behind her, without looking back, she fumbled and clawed for the edges of the tear of the brick wall canvas, and with a single violent wrench, tore another huge section away, allowing light to spill into the room.

She thought of what Winsome had said about the other side of the wall, of how the very canvas she had fallen through could have been worth a fortune. *Well, too late for that now.* She felt the tough fabric of the cloth and twisting the edge around her fist, tore again at the hole. Right now, she needed light more than she needed money, now, she needed to see.

What she saw left her stunned. Whether it was the knock to the head, the stress of the day or standing too quickly, her head seemed instantly to spin. As if her eyes saw every surface, taking it in in one huge gulp. The paintings were a wonder and Ruby considered whether, for the first time in her life, she was truly feeling what people described as religious awe.

Awe she thought, within the awful.

Upon every surface, stretched from ceiling to floor, were paintings of figures, so in-twined, so detailed, hellishly lifelike and terrifyingly complex.

They twisted together in their intricate tangle of poses, and the years needed for a painter to accomplish the feat, stunned her into silence.

The faces of the figures all together, screamed. Their eyes, fixed in terror, on the vast, unending enormity of nothing. Within and between each soul, skewered and chewed by this composition, was that same barren, desert of black that had assaulted Ruby since she first lay eyes on her Uncle's portrait.

It covered the walls so that the figures seemed to swim out of it, like drowning men in the sea at night. There was something, something in the tormented terror of those eyes that made hot tears well in Ruby's own. It was so, pitifully, hopeless.

To say that the walls were not weirdly beautiful, of a skill level seemingly beyond mortal man, was impossible, but so too was it to look upon them.

Ruby Murat tried and found that she couldn't, not all at once. It was beyond her physicality, to lay her eyes upon them for more than a few seconds. True, they were beautiful, but they were also, viscerally, revolting.

Looking even for a second, made her gag and heave, as if the very organs, bolted to escape. Above the seas of the damned portraits, muted icons stood.

On many the head and torso had been partially overcome, lines and swarms of insects, writhing like strange black veins over the musculature so that though still, they seemed in a way, to sink, into great pools of viscous ink.

What stung more, more than these forced, craven poses, was every figures' lack of eyes. For the whole of the eye, in almond width, had been painted over, totally black with a single, awful colour rendered emptily, endlessly, blank.

Someone or something had stolen their light. Plucked, removed or vanished over, all that was good and right about them and its place it had left only nought. A nothing as empty as void can be. In the end it was this, more than the rest, that forced from Ruby the half-digested contents of her guts.

Wiping her mouth and recoiling in disgust from the vomit, Ruby walked, apprehensively, toward the centre of the room. There, facing toward the tattered entrance, was a single canvas on an easel.

Again, it was covered completely from edge to edge in black. Pacing unsteadily toward it, trying as best she could to avert her eyes from the paintings, she noticed a small wooden table placed before the canvas, upon which was a leather wrap of the kind she used to hold her brushes. Her Uncle's tools, she thought.

Slowly, being careful not to drop any of the wrap's contents, she undid the clasp and allowed it to unspool onto the floor. Inside, was the most unique set of brushes Ruby had ever seen.

The handles, she guessed, were made of ivory or bone, smooth to the touch but with a finely weighted balance, like that of a throwing dart.

The set ranged from large, two-inch brushes with thick black bristles, to detail brushes of delicate thinness. What distinguished this set, however, was not the handles, but the ends.

On one end, the brushes were conventional, if expensive. Fine sculpted sable, that must have cost a fortune. On the other end, however, was something truly remarkable.

For on the opposing end of each brush, was a fine steel blade. Some were serrated, with wickedly sharp points. Some were as thin as razor blades, whilst others were thick like cleavers or jungle knives. Viewed from one end, these were the tools of a painter. Viewed from the other, the tools of a butcher. She wondered for a moment if her uncles' other use for these brushes were nearly as terrible as the first.

She began to wind the wrap back up, careful not to cut herself on the still keen blades. She held up the wrap to get a better view and saw with horror the small sliver of light begin to shrink behind her. She turned in panic and screamed unashamedly, as the great black door, slammed shut. She was in the black.

Ruby's first thought was of drowning. As if in the sea at night. When, after all the lights have gone, the ocean swells and swallows in silent privacy, giving no clues to its shape or depth. Darkness so total, it almost had form, seemed to swirl and crash around her, all dimension, width and proportion, lost in a deluge she could not see.

This sea of black that sprawled and laughed, immense and indifferent left her blind, to flail and drown.

Terror, hard and cold as ice crackled through her every nerve, as her breathing, light, fast and frantic, bit for air in short, snapped gulps. "Jesus, Jesus, Jesus" she repeated to herself over and over in a half prayer as the copper penny taste of fear filled her mouth. She stretched out her arms first at her sides and tried to assume a squatted crunch.

She inched forward, trying in vain to control her breathing. Dragging her feet as she edged in the general direction of the door. If she could reach the canvas, she could find the door, it was a straight line, all she had to do was walk.

She groped and flailed grasping at nothing, hoping for purchase, for something, an edge. Again, she moved with panicked steps—tiny movements toward the door, scared to move faster, scared to remain. Her heart thundered painfully in her chest. She paused, and reached with outstretched hands, into the darkness into the black, hoping, praying to find a surface. Finally, with only the tips of her fingers, she lightly brushed against something hard, she fumbled and felt, moving forward, searching again in the total pitch until her fingers rested, mercifully, on form, as another hand, from another body, lightly stroked her palm.

Ruby screamed, a deep, guttural, curdling scream. She snapped her hand away from the touch, and kicked and flailed, swinging wildly, trying to defend. "Get away! Get away," she screamed in terror, hitting at nothing, blind and alone.

For a moment she almost over balanced, but managed, somehow, to stay on her feet, moving now with reckless abandon, she flung herself forward toward the wall. A moment ago, it had been a few steps, now, she was running at it full pelt, filling a distance of metres and miles, nothing, nothing, just endless void. She ran and ran, until finally, sobbing, she touched her hand to the wall.

Wall? she thought, she must have mis-stepped. It had been canvas moments ago. She was in the wrong part. In there, with someone.

Groping in panic, the left and the right, she felt for canvas, a tear or an edge. Her hands skimmed upward, downward, brick, brick, cold, hard stone.

That's impossible, her mind screamed. In protest, she screamed the words aloud for no-one to hear. She fell to her knees and clambered onto all fours. For a moment, she paused and steadied her breath.

"Okay, okay. It's round here somewhere." Feeling the point where the brick met the ground, she proposed to follow the edge of the room.

"The room is a rectangle" she reassured herself. "I got turned around, but I'm going back" she sniffed hard, took a deep breath and screamed the words at the pools of black.

"There is no fucking Bogey okay? There's no-one here. Just you, alone. You on your knees and those *fucking* paintings. Now feel Ruby! Feel!" She spat the words like molten bullets.

"You are getting out." She moved, scrabbling on hands and knees, one hand scraping and jarring against the wall.

At one point she flinched as something tiny landed on her arm. She flicked it off and continued to claw around the perimeter, slowly, carefully. Again, it landed, this time on her finger. A small ticklish whisper of buzz. She flicked her hands and shuffled some more, her skinned knees grazed by the rough boards below, by her ear a small fly buzzed, as two more landed on her ear and cheek. She swatted at the darkness and still she felt. Two on her calves, one on her elbow, she could feel them landing on her neck, her scalp.

She stopped to swat but the buzzing grew louder, she spat as one landed right on her lips, tiny legs and spiky bristling hairs, landing and lightly caressing the flesh, still the buzz, and more and more, two on her eyebrow, three on her cheek, her chest, her collarbone, four on her arm. "Get off! Get off!" she screamed as she crawled, feeling as she did, them, crawl on her, hundreds and hundreds of miniscule legs, soft vibrations of a plump little thorax, around her mouth, the corners of the eyes, into her nostril, she snorted and brushed, but to no avail. More and more and closer they buzzed, they were everywhere, her left knee, nose, shoulder, and throat.

Again, she screamed and thrashing, rose to her feet swiping madly at things unseen. She turned to the wall and banged her fists, as Winsome had earlier against the stone, the pads of her hands bruising instantly. Screeching wildly, she screamed at the wall "Lemme out!" she cried "You bastard let me out!" She felt flies crawling all over her scalp, her hairline, her eyelids, and as her fist pierced through the canvas, she fell once more, into the light.

Chapter Seven

She slid through the hole like a baby deer, escaping the stomach of some great snake. Slick with sweat and pulling with her hands, she heaved herself, headfirst, down a few stairs. Her bruised legs trailed behind her as she kicked and flailed. Finally out, she sat and sobbed and cried with an anguish of fear and relief. Finally, later, she sat, on the staircase, five from the top, her back propped against the wall and her knees pulled up.

Most of what happened she could explain. *The door had swung shut, loose on its hinges and forced by a draft. That made the room so hopelessly black. In her confusion, she'd gotten turned around, and reached for something that seemed to touch back. Probably the brushes, or the edge of the stool. Then she'd run in circles, losing her bearings and going over the same space time and again. Then, in her panic, she'd disturbed the flies that had been nesting up there, feasting on something rotten, and they had reacted. That's all there was to it.* She hadn't really convinced herself of these explanations, but there had to be one. Yes, there had to be an explanation. Her thoughts turned from panic to denial to help steady her nerves.

51

Her mind flippantly resolved to bring a big can of fly spray and a spotlight if she got the nerve to visit the attic again. Maybe have an exterminator go in first.

Eventually, she raised her head and staring up, looked back at the doorway "How'd you explain *that* then Ruby? Do you *really* think so?" she bitingly hissed at herself as the new, unwanted, unwelcome realization came.

The door itself remained wide open, exactly where she had left it sometime before. It *was* plausible that it could have swung shut again, with the draft. But, heavy as the door was, it seemed incredibly unlikely that the door would swing shut, then voluntarily, swing open again. Ruby pelted down the stairs.

***

If the sun had likewise risen in Northern Scotland, Ruby hadn't noticed. Perhaps the black had bled into grey, the house become lighter, but the layer of cloud clung to the night as if reluctant to let the day arrive. Seated at the kitchen table, her still shaking hands wrapped around a mug of strong coffee, she glanced up at the clock and sighed heavily, catching as she did a glimpse of her reflection, distorted and lengthened in the chrome teapot that also sat on the table. A single curl of her hair, still damp with the residual sweat of panic, was plastered, to the centre of her forehead.

There was no point trying to sleep. Her mind swam with images, flat depictions in woodcuts of bearded men with heavy sacks, carrying off children as their mother's sobbed, of sacred faces, marred and changed by soot coloured paint and of disfigured tortured people with black empty eye sockets.

Turning her palm upward she tried to examine the bites on her triceps which was throbbing and sting as if she had been jabbed with some sharp steel object. She had goose-bumps all over her body. She glanced at the clock— 5.45 am.

At nine the man would be here to deliver *her things* from the mainland. Items. That, she had told herself—that— would help her make this space, this haunt, her own. When she had pictured herself putting up ornaments, hanging paintings and putting, her 'own unique stamp' upon the place, she hadn't imagined she'd be sharing it. She shuddered at the thought.

"I'm not sharing this house," she said out loud, unsure, even as she said it, whether she was simply refusing to share or dismissing the possibility that there was someone else there. Someone or something.

Rodger stirred and rising to his feet, curled around Ruby's legs reassuringly. She leant down to scratch his head and inexplicably, felt herself getting teary. *It's just tiredness*. Though that fact of it was, she knew, it was something else. She hoisted Rodger bodily onto her lap.

"That's right Rodge. I'm already sharing, aren't I?" She sighed and scratched his ears for a few moments before, lifting him onto the table then downed the remnants of her coffee and, pushing back the chair to stand up.

The room was definitely lightening now and whether it was the coffee, the departure of the dark, or Rodger's unconditional affection, she felt once again that surge of stubborn determination. Padding barefoot to the door of the kitchen, she stared straight across the hall, through the opposite doorway and at the hideous portrait of her uncle and his shadow.

Rodger, who had been reluctant to depart his seat on the lap, came to her side and sat by her right leg. She glanced down, then back at the painting—at the eyes, the beard, the shadow and the black. Finally, feeling the words boil up from somewhere in her chest, never taking her eyes from the portrait she again spoke aloud.

"Listen to me you bastard. This is our house now and you're going to have to do a damn sight better than that to get rid of me." She raised her hand and pointed at the painting." Tomorrow, I'm going to clean myself up and then, damnit, I'm going to paint." She jumped as two floors above her, the door to the attic slammed shut. Ruby shuddered, walked to the hall rack and lifted her coat from the hook.

Traipsing through the sodden grass of the heath towards town Ruby relaxed, the thought of fresh coffee and warm food spurring her forward. The morning was chill, yet the sun coloured the horizon with a watery blush of orange and pink, that peeked out momentarily from sombre grey clouds. She considered for a second telling Mrs Neet about the previous night. There was something in the woman's coddled woollen warmth, that was supremely maternal.

She wondered how Mrs Neet would react if she heard about the shape in the curtains, the wall that wasn't there and that touch. That awful, gentle touch. The things she'd seen in the attic and the things that she hadn't. She decided not to tell her. A comforting breakfast would have to do.

To Ruby's infinite relief, the chair by the counter was unoccupied this morning. Mr Neet being either still in bed, or otherwise engaged.

Despite it being morning, the ashen sky made it necessary to use electric lights and lit by a warm, yellow, bulb the store once again glowed like a lighthouse or beacon. An island in the dark.

Behind the counter, wrapped as ever in a thick woollen cardigan Mrs Neet greeted her with rosy cheeks glowing roundly like autumn apples.

"Mornin' dearie" she said, half stooped and busying herself with something beneath the counter.

"Morning" said Ruby weakly. Realising as she did, that was she was struggling to hold back tears. She couldn't help it. The warmth, the cheer, the insulation of the place, of her, felt like such a counterpoint, that the feelings threatened to overwhelm her. She coughed, and swallowing hard, supressed the tears.

From beneath the counter Mrs Neet produced two mugs and a squat teapot swaddled in a tea-cosy that matched the colour of her cardigan. She caught Ruby's eyes and smiling, gestured with a nod towards the pot.

"Lets 'ave a cuppa eh"? She said pouring the steaming liquid into a mug. She motioned toward the armchair and handed a mug to Ruby. Ruby was not accustomed to this treatment. In London, a visit to the shop was transactional. There might, at best, be a cheery 'hullo' or polite 'good morning' but never an offer of tea, an invitation to sit, to be. Collapsing into the chair Ruby realised with a hollow pang of loneliness that it wasn't just the contrast she felt. This warmth, this offer, this acceptance, wasn't just missing from shopping. It was never there. Despite herself, Ruby Murat, began to cry.

With the tears came the story. All the events of the night before flooding damply from her. Mrs Neet listened attentively, periodically taking large slurping gulps of tea. At the end of the narrative, wild and implausible, there was a long pause. Mrs Neet pressed her lips together.

"Hmmm.." she began. "There's always been somethin' 'bout that house." She sighed and with a swat of her hands, as if batting away her darker ruminations, smiled.

"Still, there's be no such things and ghosts and bogeys. You been listening to me old fella too hard." Ruby bowed her head. She had never mentioned how chillingly similar the old man's croaky nursery rhymes had been to her own grandmother's demon. She sniffed, at once embarrassed but also relieved to have told someone the things she barely believed herself.

"The thing is, my lovely, by the sounds of things you've had a hell of a few months." Ruby nodded, still staring at the floor. her hands clasped around the tea. "It's a long journey up from that London, you've had no sleep and nerry a bite to fill yer belly. It's no wonder yer frazzled. I mean that house..." she started to laugh through her words and placed a cool, but comforting hand on the back of Ruby's own, "I mean look at it for Pete's sakes, it's enough to give anyone heebie jeebies." Ruby herself laughed at this and taking Mrs Neet's offer of a handkerchief, dabbed at her eyes.

"Thank you." She said croakily.

"Oh, don't mention it, love. There's nothing a nice spot tea cannae help with. You'll see, once you make the place your own, it'll be grand."

They talked some more, about London and her work. She told her about Rodger, whom Mrs Neet insisted on seeing photographs of and made Ruby promise she would bring down to meet her. They talked about Winsome and about Pete, and how life gave you massive lows sometimes and a swept you high at others.

Eventually Ruby thanked Mrs Neet again and said that she needed to get back to meet the man from the removal company delivering her things from London.

"Now you be sure to unpack those things and see a bit of yoursel' up there." said Mrs Neet , packing a large paper bag with the foodstuffs Ruby had requested. Without thinking, Ruby lifted the small child's exercise book that had been lying on the arm of the chair and began to flick through it.

It was pleasingly naïve scattered with crayola drawings of seemingly eclectic images. A lion and a motorcar beneath which were letter shapes and words, written over and over. Clearly cursive writing practice. Here and there a red tick gave encouragement or corrected a spelling. On one page, joined lines of the letter 'c' moved across the page like the crests of waves, whilst on another, the lines of Little Miss Moffatt had been written in a careful cursive hand. "Along came a spider that sat down beside her and frightened Miss Muffat away." Beneath the writing exercise was a drawing of the offending arachnid, a huge red smiley face with a crop of spindly legs that made it look suspiciously similar to the sun from a few pages earlier. Ruby grinned. A budding artist, she thought.

"I take it these aren't Mr Neet's" she ventured, holding up the book and smiling broadly.

"Ach no." Mrs Neet laughed," Those are our Evie's exercises. They're years old, I found them just the now when I was cleaning out back here. She's away to the university now. She's bright as a button so she is."

"Yeah, I can see" said Ruby flicking idly through the pages. At the last two pages her smile dropped.

At the top of the first was a crudely drawn man, his beard made of massive swirls. In his hand, was a sack from which the lollipop head of a smaller stick figure was peeping. The face was frowning, and the arms held desperately aloft. A child in a sack.

Below the drawing, in the same innocent hand was the rhyme, "Old Bogey hums in the moving black" the rest of the rhyme was missing, but the adjacent page had been scribbled over. Furiously coloured in black crayon. Ruby felt the fear clutch once again at the pit of her stomach.

"I've put you in a few candles lovey, looks like a big storm tonight and sometimes the power goes out."

Ruby stared at where Evie had written the rhyme and at the thinly scrawled corrections in red. Where she had written Bogey, someone had put a careful red line through and above, neatly printed the correction.

"Old '*Auggy*' hums on the moving black." Ruby gasped in a loud involuntary gulp, the connection was not lost on Ruby.

"Hopefully you won't be needin' 'em," went on Mrs Neet, "but you never know. If you get scared, you come down here. You dinnae want to be up there on your own in the dark."

"No." Whispered Ruby. "I don't."

Chapter Eight

The trudge uphill, back to the house, was a lonely one. The hint of colour had disappeared, replaced by a layer of fog that cloaked the horizon. From the path, Ruby could faintly make out the shape of the house and, when a patch of fog cleared, she saw the top of the house emerge, with the great tree and the downturned V line of the attic roof. The attic with its one, black, window, seeming to hang in the air, it gave the impression of floating menacingly above the wreaths of cloud.

Ruby glanced back toward town, the store was now just a haze of yellow. A splintered jewel like a streetlight viewed through a rain-soaked windscreen. Turning, Ruby clutched the bag to her chest and moved reluctantly towards the house.

Over and over in time with her steps, Ruby played the awful rhyme, casting her mind back to her grandmother's face, that hand, that voice. Had she, could she have been saying 'Auggy' all along and if so, had she been referring to Auguste, the uncle Ruby never knew?

Never had the possibility occurred to Ruby that her grandma had said "Our Auggy" because they actually had one.

Lost in thought and watching her steps, careful not to slip on slicks of mud, Ruby glanced up at the house and froze. There, before the door, half hidden by the fog was the outline of a man. That's fine, she thought. I'm expecting a man. It was only as she got closer, that she noticed the sack.

Hastening her steps, she called through the grey hoping to hear some normal, human response. To Ruby's relief a voice called back.

"Hello," the voice called. "Is this your house?" As she got closer the figure came into view. A man of maybe thirty five or forty years old. He had ginger hair, a scruffy beard and implausibly— considering the chill— was wearing a short sleeved blue polo shirt. Ruby had been right about one thing. In his left hand he was clutching a sack. In his right arm he held Rodger.

Ruby, who was certain she had left Rodger safely inside was startled and bundling her bag onto the stoop moved forwards to take him. The man, still holding Rodger firmly, pulled apprehensively away.

"This your cat is it?" He said, working his wrist as Rodger squirmed within his grasp.

"Yes. I'm sorry he must've gotten out. Come on Rodge," she called as Rodger wrestled free and seemingly in one movement, leapt from the man's arms and back to Ruby's side.

"Aye he's gotten out, because I let him out. The poor thing was yowling for his life."

Ruby, who had bent to scoop up the feline glared up at him.

"I'm sorry. How did you let him out? More importantly how did you get into my house to let him out?" The man stepped back and angrily holding up the sack, pointed at Rodger.

"I havenae been in your house," he snapped angrily "When I got here this was nailed to your door." He again held up the sack accusingly "The cat was inside – his legs were bound up tight an rope cuttin' in an all."

***

Over the next two hours the man helped to unload Ruby's belongings, brought by tractor and dolly truck from where the ferry docked, and helped her to stack them haphazardly in the kitchen.

Throughout this process, carried out in an icy, agonizing silence, the issue of Rodger's discovery hung between them like an invisible barrier. Now and again, she would catch him looking at her from the corner of his eye, a faint but definite undercurrent of accusation in the glance. Ruby felt a knot of resentful indignation tighten within her chest. *He thinks I did that. That I would do that.* She pushed her anger into moving the boxes and despite the chill of the morning broke a sweat through the exertion.

Recognising one particular box that had been placed on the table, she plunged, elbow deep into the assortment of items, rummaging for one thing in particular. For a moment she thought of herself reaching in the dark, of the fingers that with a whisper's breath had grazed her own.

Soon however, her hands clasped the pleasing thickness of a paint tube and she smiled, sighing with relief and happiness.

The tube, she knew was titanium white, larger than all of her other tubes and the length of a small ruler, it felt cool and substantial in her hand. Imbued, she thought, with a strength in its opacity. She longed to daub and spread it, with liberal thickness, to feel the slight, yielding resistance of its texture on canvas. Soon, she thought nodding silently to herself.

She lifted the box of materials off the table and clutching it awkwardly in front of her, carried it toward the living room where she intended to set up her easel and, once the man was gone, she would use them. Ruby's mind wandered back to moment she had found the brushed upstairs, and the feel of svelte softness of the sable tips and in contrast, the steely sharpness of the blades. Shuddering at what imagined Auguste had done with those blades, she pushed the thought aside and she shifted her hip to better support the weight of the box, then paced toward the hall.

As she reached the door, she saw the man standing, his arms hanging limply by his sides in the doorway of the living room. His back was to her and he was staring, just as she had the previous day, transfixed on the portrait.

Ruby coughed loudly in an effort to disturb him, to drag him back to the here and now. Slowly, he turned toward her. Immediately she could see, there were tears in his eyes. Fixing his eyes on hers, he opened his mouth to speak and stalled. He swallowed deeply and, wiping the tears from his eyes and dropped his gaze, muttering softly,

"It were God awful, that what happened, like — to your cat." He phrased this as a statement, a terrible blank realisation hitting him. Terrible but true.

Lifting his head, he stared solidly this time, into Ruby's eyes, as if trying, silently to communicate why, how, he knew. Ruby stared back, and gently shook her head.

The man moved hurriedly toward the door, twice pushing desperately before realising that the door swung inwards, he pulled in panic at the handle with revealing haste and tottered hurriedly down the steps. Making sure that he was several paces from the house before he slowed.

Eventually, he came to a stop. Pausing with his back to the house as if, having forged an instinctive retreat, he'd hit some barrier of conscience, of duty or honour that stopped him from running headlong into the safety of the heath, the human overruling the animal.

He stood, like a scarecrow, rooted to the spot as Ruby, with her painter's eye for composition, noticed that the point at which he had stopped was two steps out from the shadow of the house. Without turning around, he spoke solemnly.

"You know," he stuttered "You, err...you don't *have* to stay here. You're welcome to stay at mine, I mean..." he stumbled, struggling to justify the invitation, even to himself. Ruby didn't flinch. "I've got spot here, in town, for when I stay on the island – it's small, but you'll be a'right."

In what context, in what world, would such an invitation, from a complete stranger ever be normal? Under what pressures, what circumstances, would such a human man decide, that he needed to offer her sanctuary? What was it about this house and the things that hid within it that made it seem so hostile, to make him think that escape was the only option? She didn't need an answer.

She was still in the shadow. Reaching into the box she had placed by her feet, she grabbed the tube of paint.

"Thanks," she said, to the man's back. "But I'm not going anywhere." Rodger had been sitting by the wheel of the truck, refusing to return to the interior of house. "Come on Rodge." She moved to pick him up, but he ran. The man turned to Ruby.

"Seems he dinnae want to go back. If ye want, I'll take him for a while. Till ye get it sorted."

Chapter Nine

Alone again, except for Rodger shut in his cage, she stood, as he had stood, in doorway of the living room. Draped across a straight-backed armchair, where the man had flung it, was the sack. It was made from a coarse jute weave and had been dyed black. She played with the business card in her hand. The man, Lucas Ables, so the card informed—said to call if she felt she needed to. For a moment, she wondered whether the sack was large enough to accommodate a child. She considered the dimensions needed for such an operation—abduction, kidnap, murder. Forcing out the thought, revolted that she had even allowed it to seep into her mind, she lifted the sack and turned it over in her hands. Someone had left this sack and placed Rodger into it and bound him cruelly. The same someone was watching.

She had her explanations of course. What if, this man had lied. Known of the folklore and decided to play on it, to make a joke at her expense. But his anger at the cruelty to Rodger and desperation upon seeing the painting had already convinced her that wasn't true. Perhaps some barbaric neighbourhood boys had done it as a lark.

She even thought for a moment of Winsome, trying by increments to scare her away, to claim the attic and its value for himself. Though with his battered hands she doubted he'd be capable.

All were possibilities, all of them were rational. None of them, she knew, were the truth.

She stared at the painting. This was her audience. The shadow, with its wicked pearl white teeth grinning in infinite malice. Ruby didn't smile. Instead, the sack still in hand, she marched back into the kitchen and found her phone. After entering Lucas Able's phone number she rummaged through a number of boxes and emerged with what she sought.

In her youth it had taken her hours to perform the action she planned, now, with the help of a few steel pins and a pair of kitchen scissors she made light work of the task. With an acidic defiance, she hammered the pins in place, used a wedge for stretching, and, lifting her work for inspection strode again to living room.

The canvas frame was a small one. Smaller than she would ever work with for a final piece. She had packed several with the intention of using them for rough work, studies or sketches that would inform a final painting. Now, instead, she propped the frame on the easel that she hastily, deliberately raised in front of the portrait.

Now she stood, paints and brushes under her arm and glared purposefully at the painting.

"Watch this, you contemptable fuck" She hissed through her teeth. She ran her hand across the rough textured surface considering how the paint would adhere to it.

In his house in Arles, the yellow house he shared with Gaugin, Vincent Van Gogh had painted masterpieces. Unable to pay for canvas he'd stretched jute across the frames. Jute he'd taken from sacking.

"If it's good enough for Van Gogh, it's good enough for me."

The black sacking intended to scare, to intimidate and shake her, stretched across the frame like an empty expanse. With a single murderous slash Ruby Murat wounded it's brooding surface with colour, a flash of white across its skin. Swiping with paint, no shape, just colour, she gauged and scraped the surface, slathering reds and plastering yellows. With force and fury, she screamed at the image, making her own mantra of solidity.

"I am going nowhere."

Pausing, breathless, she stared at the shadow and looked past Auguste, into his soul, into the shadow, she glared at the smile, at the glowing the furious eyes and watched them, watching her. Ruby screamed as they moved.

There was no doubt, no question or hesitation. It had happened. Those eyes, swollen and bulbous white, like peeled hard boiled eggs had rolled to settle on Ruby and her protest.

She didn't wait. Careering forward, the easel and paints crashing to the ground she lunged at the painting, gripped the outer edges of the frame and lifted.

As a veteran of gallery shows, exhibits and shifting of her own work, she had moved many a canvas over the years. She knew instinctively the weight of a painting, of a frame and how much effort or exertion was needed to lift it from the wall.

This time, she was wrong. As if, hidden in the black there were hunks of lead, the painting ached and yawned toward the earth, its gravity and weight far beyond what it should have been.

Ruby didn't care. Doubt had been removed. He was here, he'd seen her here and he meant her harm.

With a wrenching pull that sent hot, tugging flames up the side of her body, her muscles tightening awkwardly against the strain, she twisted her hip, planted her feet and pulled. This was no trick of the eye, no phantom violin. This thing was solid, real, tangible and moveable.

With a final thrust, barking with a scream that seemed to come more from her clenched teeth than her throat, she tore the portrait from the wall and, holding its impossible weight for a fraction of a second, dropped it heavily to the floor. It teetered for a moment, balancing on the bottom edge of the frame before finally, definitively, it fell, face down.

Panting and again washed in a beading of sweat, she stared down at the back of the frame, laying on the floor like the corpse of an idea. 'Fuck Winsome' she thought. If he wants to look at it, he can lift it himself. She rose to her full height, her fingers tingling numb with adrenaline. She looked hurriedly around the room, searching the corners, checking the shadows that were already lengthening. Feeling in that awful stillness the threat or memory of movement. Her eyes darted. Ceiling to floor, wall to wall, searching, feeling for the silent, prowling terror. She turned hurriedly to where the painting had been, still scouring every surface for the something, someone that she knew, could feel, was there.

"Show yourself you bastard." She muttered. It was then that she noticed the hole.

For a moment she hesitated, watching the dark circle, this wound in the wall as if expecting something to crawl from within, a spider, with thick cigar like legs or a snake with glistening obsidian scales. Scared to fix her attention on a single point, she continued to turn tracing circles and searching, scared, she knew, to leave her back exposed, to allow any blindspot from which a thing could pounce. Nothing.

And yet, she knew. Knew as certainly as she had that the house had expected her, as surely as she had that she was being watched. She knew, and believed, there was something there and in the hole something she needed to see.

She stared at the gap, that yawning aperture, wholly unknown. Slowly, still feeling eyes upon her, despite there being nobody there, she allowed her hand, to edge, by degrees toward it.

In tiny increments, inch by inch, closer and closer before, with a quick, decisive jolt she plunged her hand within and clasped the object inside, pulling dust masonry and memories with her as he jerked it free and out.

She spun quickly, to face the room and feeling in any position, the vulnerability at her back, she backed into the corner. She pressed her spine, her potential blind spot, to the wall, and slid slowly down to sit.

She pulled up her knees and with a concentration she physically felt, searched the space of the room again.

For a moment, she considered that she should have felt the power shift, that now, at this vantage point, commanding a view of every angle, she should feel that she had taken the role of the hunter. That was not the case. And though she could see what was coming, she, she knew, was cornered.

The storm outside was gathering force. The wind whistling as it raced by the eaves as if rushing away reluctant even to touch the house. As Mrs Neet had predicted, the storm was coming. Ruby prayed that her other prediction, of power outages and needing to use candles would not be equally as accurate.

Seated on the floor her back pressed into the corner, Ruby again scanned the room. If something else was coming she'd see if when it did. If it was hunting her, she'd see it as it stalked, and marked its approach. There'd be no sneaking up, no stealthy surprise. The bastard could face her head on. This prey would be hard to hunt.

She looked down at the object she had torn from the hole and held, guardedly to her chest. She'd known at once, by touch alone, that it was a book. Wrapped around in a thick cotton cloth, she could feel the edges of its binding and the space where the cover met the pages. Removing this veil, she placed the volume on her lap and with a final check around the room glanced down at the cover. They say that a picture says a thousand words. The cover said it all.

The tome itself was bound in a hard-thick leather. On the cover, embossed into this material as if carved into it, was Leonardo's Vitruvian Man.

The drawing, which her gran had always referred to as 'that octopus one' on account of the multiple arms and legs used by Da Vici to show the proportions of the human body as described by Vitruvius, showed an angry looking man standing with his legs apart to form a triangle and his arms outstretched at shoulder height. At the other compass points extra limbs extended to show how the body, in different extensions, fit into a circle within a square. In this rendering, the man, his limbs and the shapes around were simply stamped on the black surface, details gouged into the night.

This, however, was not all.

Overlaid, on top of this famous image, painted in gold and intersecting the limbs of the man, fitting in the same measured proportions was a biological drawing of a fly, its eyes framing the head of the man, whilst its wings, folded and pointing downward mirroring the angle of the legs.

The effect of these two disparate organisms, placed together in symbolic synergy, turned Ruby's stomach and slipping a finger under the cover she opened the book at random at a random page.

The room had grown dark as the clouds gathered outside blocking the sun as Auguste Murat had done to the window upstairs, the last rays of light caught in its opaque blanket. Despite the fading light she was able to make out the images and text. Pausing every few seconds to glance nervously around the room, jumping in reflex every time the thunder clattered without, she began to read.

Ruby flicked through the pages. Leaf after leaf of hideous sketches and copious, closely written notes.

On one page, was a portrait, drawn in ink of young boy of maybe nine years old. Beneath it another of a younger but equally well drawn girl. Under both, leaking off the bottom of the page was an image of the child laying prostrate with a dark sack lying close by. They were clearly dead, with clouds of flies circling over the body.

On the opposing page written in English and, it seemed to Ruby, in the same, beautiful hand that had scribed the letter that brought her here, were notes, seemingly of scholarly intent. Ruby read a few sentences.

"At Ekron of the desert, barren to the lord, offerings were placed to Baal zebul, prince of the wilderness. And they did take fruit and flesh for the flies, making unto them a sacrifice, that they may receive the years. In the sacred name of Adoni zevooveem, were sons of men so consumed by flies." Pharisees 2:17

On another page in the same flowing hand was written

"..prevalent amongst many desert cultures the practice of 'Similar dhubabat' involves placing the first cut of meat from any slaughtered animal in a designated point 'for the flies'. As well as having the practical purpose of attracting insects and keeping them from the main meal, this tradition was thought to stem from an earlier belief that sacrifice could bestow youth..." Ruby flipped, each page it seemed, featured a collage of quotes, extracts and textual references

She turned again to where a group of loose leaves had been pressed between the pages. Removing the first, she examined it closely.

The photograph, sepia tinted and clearly of some age, showed a group of men, each wearing hooded cowls like those of a monk. They were in a dark room that closely resembled the attic. The men held in their hands, cupped before them, hunks of what looked like offal. Hearts and intestines, huge dripping flanks of meat, held aloft in triumph.

The last man standing to the right was clearly Auguste Murat, holding a paint brush in his hand. And standing next to him was a young boy. But it was that young boy that made her eyes go wide. He had misshapen hands and those eyes—she knew those eyes—they belonged to Winsome. Groping in the pocket of her jeans, she fished with difficulty, her phone from inside. Her fingers trembling, the implications of the photo and the paintings in the attic swirling in her mind, she hurriedly typed a message.

"I think I need help."

Chapter Ten

Outside, the wind was gathering force. Rain, like thrusts of iron nails, jabbed at the windows and roof, thrumming hard against them with constant drilling streams, hammering the surface as if driving ever downward to pierce the tiles and enter. The room had darkened further, in line with the sky and she knew without looking that outside the clouds hung in ferocious black.

Without standing Ruby again surveyed the room, looking, watching and searching for someone else. She instinctively looked back at the frame that she had taken down from the wall. The frame was now propped upright against the wall, but the painting was not visible—only a blank canvas stared back at her.

Someone was in the house and had stolen the painting. Despite the obvious danger she found herself in, her first thought was 'good riddance" to that ugly painting. In the next instant, her mind was flooded with alarm. She had to get out of the house. Her only thoughts were to grab Roger and get out.

As she scrambled to her feet, out of the corner of her eye, she saw something in the hole that the book had come from.

Something white, fluttering as if in a breeze—perhaps more photos or text that could help explain more of the dark history of this house. Without a second thought, she reached into the hole, groping around to quickly grab the object she had seen. Unsuccessful, she started to remove her hand, and then screamed.

As she started to pull her hand out, she felt something grip her wrist. Her immediate reaction was to try to pull her hand out quickly, but it wouldn't budge. it seemed the harder she pulled, the tighter the grip on her wrist. *Get a hold on yourself* she thought, trying to will away the rising panic. Something must have shifted in the hole—a brick perhaps, that reduced the size of the hole. As she twisted her hand and continued to pull, she an excruciating pain moved up her hand and into her wrist. The pain, a mix of pressure and burning, crawled across her fingers like fire. The feeling though, was now unmistakable——something in the hole had grabbed her wrist and it wasn't letting go.

Desperate to remove her hand from the hole, she pulled harder, feeling a pressure crushing in fingers that now spread to her hand. Still she pulled, tugging and wrenching, not caring what damage she might be doing. Ruby felt caught, as though the hole, the wall, the house itself, sought to hold her in place. Then she felt her hand being pulled in further into the hole.

Bawling and screeching in terror and pain, she kicked in panic, fighting not to go down into the gullet of this dark house. Then behind her, in the door of the room she heard a voice call her name. "Hello Ruby." She turned and gaped at the apparition. Auguste Murat had stepped out of the portrait and was standing before her. Blind terror seized her.

She gaped at him, and back to the blank canvas that sat in the frame where once the portrait of Murat had been. Her mind raced in terror, and she opened her mouth to scream, but her voice could only muster a desperate whimper as she saw the huge black sack draped across his forearm.

When she found her voice, she screeched, "No! No! Nooo!" wailing and struggling to no effect. Spinning on her backside, kicking her feet at Auguste's approach, she felt her hand go completely numb as she turned. Thrashing with terror, agony and rage, she flailed with nails, aiming to tear and defend herself as Auguste, smiling his white toothed grin, padded softly and sweetly toward her.

"Hush now. Hush now Ruby," he crooned and cooed as he inched ever closer. Taking one edge of the sack in his teeth he slipped his hand into its opening, stretching the fabric to form another dark hole, he held it gently above her head

"No! No!" She screamed as she fought. Still the sack writhed into place.

With the sack clenched in his teeth, Auguste lisped his comforting hiss "Shh, come now. It's time.'' The sack's rim, wide as her shoulders, gaped, folded, slipped over her head, with her free hand she tried to push it away, clutching the outside, pushing, clawing as Auguste sang, "Old Auggy hums in the moving black…"

The edges of the sack gripped her shoulder, tightening and clasping as if it were alive, like the throat attached to the mouth in the wall, it squirmed and swallowed in slow undulations, a muscular hold of oesophageal rings.

It swelled and contracted in sweet peristalsis sliding and itching further along, over her body as darkness, black sucked at her head, her shoulder, her chest. She tried to scream, to call, to shout. Through the jute she felt Auguste's hands cushion her head, pulling the sacking down past her waist. "To take you away in his big black sack..."

***

She awoke in darkness. Darkness and pain. At first, disoriented, she wondered where she was, though even before her eyes adjusted, somewhere deep down, she knew.

She was positioned face up and prostrate on the bare wood floor of the attic, her limbs which somehow no longer seemed to belong to her, spread in a five-point star, pinned to the floor by heavy, invisible, terrible gravity—a weight of black. There were no restraints, nothing to hold her down, and yet, try as she might she could not move a muscle. Ruby was paralysed, yet she heard, saw, smelled and felt everything.

Feeling had returned to her hand. Her fingers to the first knuckle on her left hand felt wet and cool, and itchy. *'I'm the next portrait'* she thought to herself.

As her eyes attuned to the dark, other eyes watched her, all of them impotent, powerless to help. The faces of the paintings lost in the black, peered and begged from their own private hells.

She was with them, lost in the black well, in that blackest of shades that shouldn't exist. She tried again to scream or move, but like in a dream she still stayed, entirely, helplessly pinned. Had she been injured?

Her spinal cord somehow cut during a struggle she couldn't remember, or perhaps Murat had dropped her on her way up the stairs, breaking her neck. For a moment she considered the image of Auguste, crouching over her unconscious body a pair of garden shears or pliers in hand, slowly approaching the flesh at the nape of her neck, his hands to the wrists smeared with blood as he snipped and severed the cord himself like a spiteful child cutting the strings of a marionette or a gardener clipping the stem of a rose.

No, she thought. That can't be it. I can still feel. My nerves work, it's my muscles that don't. Drugs maybe? Some nightmarish cocktail of chemicals designed to render the victim defenceless but still conscious, able to feel. She tried in vain but couldn't scream.

She tried to close her eyes, to shut out the attic, the house, the world and realised with horror that she couldn't. She was unable to blink. Her eyes, fixed, forever open, yielded now to the dark. Through the jaundiced light thrown by candles she could just about see enough to reveal edges, shapes. A dark shape lay to her left, somewhat hazy and fuzzy. As she stared, she could make out the general shape as that of a body lying unmoving on the floor.

To her horror, she realized that the fuzziness of the body's outline was due to a living blanket of thousands of flies. As her senses slowly began registering her surroundings, the steady drone of buzzing now made its way to her consciousness, along with an eye-watering stench.

Using an inner strength, she ignored the pain in her hand and the assault on her other senses and focused her mind on her situation. This must be supernatural, she thought.

Some curse or spell, some wicked pact made by wicked people to give them the power to stay here beyond their time. She had read once that fate and destiny flowed like water and through supernatural means, the flow could be diverted, like someone placing their hand into a stream changing the course momentarily, forcing the flow in another direction. At the time she had thought it nonsense, now, she was not so sure.

Her eyes, lolled and rolled in their sockets, darting like those of a fright-stricken horse. As tears streamed down her cheek, she realized she could move her eyes but couldn't close them. She had read once that tears cried as a result of different emotions looked different under a microscope, that scientists could look at tears wrought from joy or pain and tell them apart. She imagined for a second the jagged spines of what tears of terror might look like. In times of extreme stress, it is strange how one's mind darts from one disconnected thought to another.

To her right, his feet just in view, Auguste sat cross legged. The room was lit with candles, the very same candles that hours earlier had been given to her by Mrs Neet as an act of kindness, of warmth.

Again, from her stomach she tried to scream, tightening the muscles, trying to force the air, the sound to escape, to rail and cry with anger and spite at the man, the thing, that had dragged her here.

In desperation, in an animal act, she snorted and blew the air from her nose. Around her, a stinking reek curled its tendrils across the room.

Pushing and fighting with all of her might, she forced the tendons of her neck to tense, to lever and lift the boulder of her head ever so slightly. To her right, Auguste sighed softly. "Oh," he said breathily, and leaning forward stroked at her hair. "You want to lift your head?" The reek grew somehow stronger, floating as if in pieces on the surface of another scent. The sickly, sweet odour of corpulent rot. "It would be good for you to see." As he spoke, Ruby's neck slowly loosened and with an effort she was able to raise and move her head.

Auguste Murat slid back toward his seated position. She could see blood pooling on the floor. For a moment she panicked thinking that perhaps the blood was hers, that, unable to feel she was slowly bleeding to death without knowing it. Glaring downward as best she could at her body, her eyes blurred with tears she could see no wounds. Looking back at Auguste, to where he sat cross legged on the floor, saw that the pool trailed back to the fly-ridden body on the floor. The blood was not hers.

Chapter Eleven

Auguste saw Ruby's eyes darting from the blood pool to the body and back at her. A slight smile flashed over his form, as understanding of what she was seeing flickered over Ruby's face. Charles Winsome 's disfigured, grotesque little body lay mutilated and quite, quite dead Just a few feet from her, the abject terror etched into the crevices of his face was chronicled on canvas in dramatic strokes of red, orange and bronze. Only deep black sockets remained where his eyes had been removed. Ruby's stomach lurched and bile rushed to her throat and pooled in her mouth. Auguste bent his head this way, and that, studying Ruby as she lay mostly paralyzed. He traced his fingers through the air sketching what Ruby knew, were the plans of her torture.

Ruby tried to summon the scream that raged in her throat, but no sound came. The skin above her knee twitched instinctively as a bluebottle landed, circled and landed again. Another landed on the soft flesh of the joint at the inside of her elbow and was edging with a slow ticklish crawl up her bicep. It was joined by another and then a third. Two came to rest on her throat, again landing hovering and returning like soft random touches.

Presumably these flies were displaced from the thousands that had somehow found their way to Winsome's fresh corpse.

An involuntary shiver quivered over her body, causing the flies to take flight and hover over her. Here in this room of untold horrors where things from nightmares lived and breathed a simple fly should never have held such import. And yet, unable to swat or crush, the awful lightness of their spiky touch held within it a naked truth. There was no escape. No resistance. As another fly, of juicy fatness landed on her cheek she screamed and sobbed at her inability to move it, to shoo it away. Prone like this, the fly would have its way.

"Ruby..." Auguste intoned, as if comforting a child. "It's almost time." From somewhere on the floor he lifted a small oval mirror in a golden frame. Streaks of candlelight shimmered across its surface as he moved. Ruby raised her head. She wanted to shout at him, to curse and spit with acid words. All she could do was scream.

In her terrified state of mind, the shades of paint on the portraits had suddenly began to move and writhe and ooze their pain in liquid form. Soon, she knew, she would be among them, painted in raw and ravaged shapes.

She felt her breath, tight and rasping cutting short her screams. Her eyes blurred with tears and flitted frantically back and forth as the black began to leak and drip, running down accursed walls and pooling like oil as it met the ground. Or she realised, as *they* hit the ground. For it wasn't paint, oil or ink that was inching flowing down the walls but millions upon millions of flies. She must be hallucinating.

Finally, from somewhere she managed to find her scream. This time, it came as a solid thing that ripped through her throat, a sound that was whole, round and vast, bigger than her lungs her throat or her mouth, primal and viscous. Her screams and cries found their edges, slowly coagulating into words

"Help! Please Jesus God. Help me. Help me. She sobbed "Please, please. No!"

Auguste Murat mewled in delight. Ruby tried to kick, to wake from the nightmare, instead she lay, rigidly still, stricken and prone. Nakedly vulnerable, she was locked in place. All she could do was scream.

Grinning with malice Auguste moved forward. His steps wet and thick on the floor, around it, flies swarmed circled him so that he seemed to be clothed in a black mass of insects. An excitement of vivid evil danced in his eyes, as he surveyed her hungrily. Her screams were stopped as she became choked and throttled by a mind that rebelled in disbelief.

Auguste slowly leaned toward her, then tittered briefly with a childish glee as he moved around behind her, just out of sight.

For a moment, there was a silence broken only by the incessant humming of flies. She strained her eyes, forcing them further than vision allowed, trying to look from the corner, to catch a glimpse and at least look death in the eye. Then, she felt his breath moving behind her head, hot and moist, fetid with decay.

Like a scavenging animal approaching a carcass, he moved slowly in long liquid movements, his face and mouth bending low. His breath upon her cheek, her throat.

She felt the muscles in her neck, flinch and twitch in anticipation of his touch. He was toying with her, leaving her weeping, tortured in terror, waiting, listening in an agony of expectation. Auguste Murat was alive again, revelling in anticipation of death and of life.

She watched Auguste's eyes and his grin towering above behind her head and as he brought the knife-edged into view and he slowly lifted it above his head.

As she looked away in anticipation of the torture to come, the agony that he would record in strokes of rabid colour—as she did this—she noticed a tiny sliver of yellow, like a single star in an empty sky. It was one of the candles Mrs Neet had given her. Its tiny light almost entirely consumed by the black. Almost but not quite. Ruby could just see her arm, stretched impotently to her left and just beyond it, the tiny pin prick of a flame.

Ruby focused on that light. The small yellow flame of colour and warmth. And even in this pit of darkness, light. The light had stayed. The colour remained, even here it burned, a tiny shard of will.

She shifted her gaze from the candle to her own hand, to her little finger and tried, tried with every ounce of her being, to make her finger move. Ruby in the final moments of defiance, forced herself to block out everything except this one thing, the ability to make her finger move.

Auguste began laughing again with a childlike mirth and continued to hum and sing. Still she stared at her finger, just a twitch, a movement, an inch, some rebellion to say and to show that *I will not succumb*.

A red-hot pain ripped through her shoulder, as her head spun to the right, drawn by the immediacy of agony. She screamed again. Forcing herself to ignore the reality of her injured flesh, she flung her head back to the left, to the light.

Auguste began to pace around to the right to observe his handiwork, humming *Old Auggy*.

Her finger twitched.

Auguste went to the wall and using the blood-smeared brush, began painting. After only a few strokes, he put the brush down, wiped it clean, then picked up another brush with a sharp blade on one end. He walked slowly back toward Ruby behind her head and knelt.

Ruby felt her fingers move and with a single jolt fastened around the shaft of the candle. "If this is hell," she spat, "then you should be fucking burning!" With a wrenching movement she swung her arm, lifting the still lit candle in a huge arc around her head until she felt the end of it connect with *something*.

There was a high-pitched squeal as the metallic clanging of the brush/knife as it fell from the hand of Murat to the floor. Ruby, struggled to pull her legs up beneath her, shifting her hips and kicking her legs, driving a swarm of flies into the air. Crawling to the portraits she set them aflame.

The grimaces of pain on the faces of the tortured souls were released as they melted into multi-coloured pools and ash. In that fearsome, terrifying, wonderful, moment, spectres of light rose from the slick oil and hovered in the orange glow.

In the light of the fire, Ruby watched the hideous face of Auguste Murat contort in horror as the apparitions descended upon his screaming, writhing, malevolent form.

It was then that a strange calm overtook her. Somewhere in space between the living and the dead, Ruby Murat heard or perhaps felt whispers surround her. Helping hands carried and lifted her onto the ledge of the window. The smashing of glass caused by the inferno roaring behind her sounded strangely soothing. She teetered on the ledge for a second then fell, gently through broken window, out of the flaming darkness into the light. As she fell, whispers of thanks followed her. Then Ruby Murat quietly lost consciousness.

Chapter Twelve

Lucas Able stood momentarily at the foot of Ruby Murat's house. He'd jumped in his truck the moment he got her text, not thinking of anything more than getting to the house as fast as he could.

But now horror paralyzed him as he watched flames gently licking through the roof of the manor house.

A sharp crack shattered the silence and Lucas watched in horror as black glass splintered down in shards and Ruby Murat tumbled from the cyclops eye.

He began to move, each movement seemingly as slow as treacle for the enormity of the task required. Whether he dreamed it or not, he could not determine, yet he was aware of being ushered along, his legs propelled forward with unseen energy, as Ruby Murat plunged to what should have been a certain death, Lucas Able broke her fall, and they both tumbled to the ground.

Epilogue

There would always be unanswered questions. Most of all for Ruby. The house razed to the ground, offered up no burned human remains – nothing remained of the fly ridden body on the floor. It was as though Charles Winsome never was. No evidence of him could be validated, no matter how thorough a search the police made. In the rubble of the fire, the frame that once held the painting of Auguste Murat lay somehow uncharred, yet the canvas was missing, as though it also, never was.

And how had Ruby escaped the blaze? If the smoke hadn't killed her, the fall should have. Had Ruby imagined it after-all? Imagined Winsome, the portraits, the hands that had helped her through the blackened window?

Her psychiatrist said it was the only plausible explanation, as he probed her with cold and clinical questions about the unexpected breakdown of her brief marriage. Ruby, he believed, was suffering hallucinations bought about by shock.

But Lucas didn't think so, and that was all that mattered to Ruby. She just needed one person to believe in her. And Lucas did, because he had been there too.

The only good thing to come out of the entirely bizarre experience of Auguste Murat's miserable legacy was Lucas. Lucas and Rodger. How Rodger survived the blaze unscathed was something even the firey's could not explain.

THE END

I hope that you enjoyed this book.

If you are willing to leave a short and honest review for me on Amazon, it will be very much appreciated, as reviews help to get my books noticed.

Over the page you will find a preview of one of my other books,

The Haunting of Crael Manor

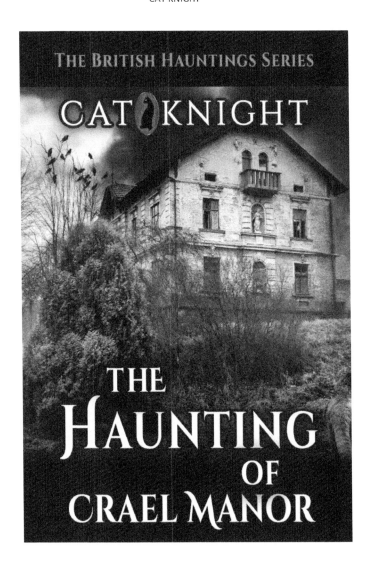

THE HAUNTING OF CRAEL MANOR

CAT KNIGHT

PROLOUGE

Clordana looked into the mirror and frowned. On her left cheek, toward her thin upper lip was a spot. She leaned closer, in an effort to determine whether the spot was on her skin or on the mirror. Old mirrors were spotted and wavy. They didn't reflect the beauty Clordana obviously displayed. She frowned and then relaxed her face. Frowning, like smiling, deepened those wrinkles. Everyone knew that.

"MAEVE!" Clordana called. "MAEVE!"

Clordana waited until her old and trusted maid shuffled into the large bedroom that had served her since she became the head of the household. The bedroom was the largest and best-appointed bedroom in the manor house. It had been her parents' bedroom when Clordana was growing up; she remembered running into the room and finding them in deep discussion. Clordana always wondered what they found to talk about. Probably finances, because finances seemed to be forever on her mind.

"Milady," Maeve said.

"Come here," Clordana said. "Look at my cheek." She leaned out. "Tell me if there is a spot next to my upper lip."

The old woman, who had served Clordana's mother, squinted. "If we could have some light," Maeve said.

"No light. I have it on the highest authority, that alabaster skin is preferred. It is a sign of proper breeding and peerage. Darkened skin is for labourers."

"Well then," Maeve said and touched Clordana's cheek. "I'd say it was spot then."

"No, no, no," Clordana said. "It can't be a spot. A spot would mean aging, and I refuse to age. Remember what the witch said? No aging as long as I follow her instructions."

"Yes, milady."

"Is one ready?"

"No, milady."

"How could there not be one ready? Didn't I give instruction that three be brought in this month."

"Three were brought in, milady."

"Then, how could there not be one to use?"

"You have used three, milady."

"I most certainly have not. This is but the ides of the month. I would not have need of three."

"It is past the ides, milady."

"It is? What is the date then?"

"The twenty-fifth."

"The twenty-fifth?"

"Yes, milady."

"That hardly seems possible. That would mean we're but one week from Autumn, and I refuse to believe that we are but one week short of the leaves changing."

"Even so, it is true, milady."

Clordana looked back at the mirror. "I know I set a limit of three, but I will not be bound by silly limits of my own making. Send them out to fetch another."

"But, Milady—"

"No buts, Maeve. I need one, and I shall have one. See to it."

Maeve hesitated, staring at the mirror.

"What is it, Maeve? Did I not make myself clear?"

"It's the villagers, milady. They have threatened to take action if any more are taken."

"Piffle. They are leeches that live off me. They will do nothing, as doing nothing is in their best interest."

"There are rumblings."

"Nonsense. Fetch me one and prepare it immediately. I will not go another day without my treatment."

"Yes, milady."

"And Maeve, make sure it's a young one this time. This spot is testament to one that was too old."

"Yes, milady."

Clordana looked into the mirror and forced her face to rid itself of any emotion. Wrinkles, wrinkles, wrinkles.

Later, Clordana stood at the window, mindful not to be in the sunlight and looked across the fields that she owned, and the townsfolk worked. The order of things had been ordained centuries before. She and hers owned, and the lesser toiled. God's will. Simple and elegant.

The scream echoed through the manor house, and Clordana frowned. That wouldn't do, it wouldn't do at all. She rose from her chair and headed for the door, even as it opened.

"Milady," Maeve said.

"Out of my way," Clordana said. "How many times have I told them about the screams. I'm afraid I must make an example of someone."

"You should leave them to their business, milady."

"And listen to that? I am not a monster, Maeve. I will not have it as long as I am mistress of Locket Manor."

Clordana passed the older woman and headed for the stairs. In moments, she had descended to the first floor. She marched into the main hall and opened the door to the cellar, to the dungeon her forebears had used to gain confessions. The torches burned, providing enough light for her to find her way. She knew it by heart. In moments, she was in the inner room, the room with the truth machines.

"Milady," Thompson said, as she entered.

"What happened, Thompson?" she asked.

"I apologise, but the scream came before we even opened the door. There was nothing I could do."

"If you weren't so loyal and adept," Clordana said, "I would put you out in a trice. But I am in a good mood, so I will but warn you. No more."

"Yes, milady."

Clordana looked at the naked girl stretched out on the rack. Clordana thought fourteen or fifteen perhaps, and not particularly pretty.

"This is the best you could do?" she asked.

"Yes, milady, the villagers were reluctant."

"Reluctant? Do I not feed them? Do I not clothe them? Do I not keep them warm when winter howls about their wretched hovels? Reluctant? They should offer their prettiest on bended knee. They should beg me to take the best. I have half a mind to return her and take another."

To Clordana, Thompson looked stricken, as if she had told him to find other employment—if he could.

"She'll do, Thompson, she'll do. Get on with it, before I change my mind."

"Will you be stayin' then?" he asked.

"For a bit, perhaps. Longer, if I feel the need."

The large, heavy man picked up a long knife. The gagged girl's eyes widened, and she fought her constraints.

"Yes," Clordana said. "Excite the blood. Make it roil."

Thompson grabbed the girl's skinny leg and pinned it down. The shiny blade flashed in the light.

"Slowly, Thompson," Clordana said. "Precision is necessary. Remember what the witch said. The cuts must be in the proper order and of the proper depth.

"Yes, milady."

Clordana watched for a few minutes, listening to the muffled screams of the girl, watching the careful cuts, mindful of the blood flowing into the bucket. Thompson did know his business, but then, he had been preparing the blood for some time. With a smile, Clordana marched out of the room and back to her bedroom. She, too, had to prepare.

"When you have enough, come to the tower," she said.

Clordana stood naked in the tower room, the highest room of the keep. Torches burned about the room, casting a wavery light over everything, although there wasn't much. The room was bare except for the font by the window, the special font with runes on its five sides. The witch had supervised the carving of the stone font. She had placed the runes in a particular order, the order that would make the spell come to life. Clordana had performed the rite many times, but even so, she was always excited when the time came. This was what she lived for—beauty.

Thompson brought the steaming blood into the room. The red mist began to flow, out of the font, down the sides, across the floor. The mist meant the magic was working. Clordana loved the mist. Maeve poured the blood into the font, making Clordana smile with excitement.

Using a painter's brush, Clordana carefully dabbed herself with the blood, in the precise places prescribed by the witch. Then, she smiled at Maeve.

"This feels so young," Clordana said. "It will make the spot go away. I'm sure of it."

"Yes, milady."

With an eager smile, Clordana lowered her face into the basin, letting the warm blood feed her hungry skin. She was immersed, eyes closed, relishing the feel.

Then, she felt the hand on the back of her head, pressing her face deeper.

What?

She tried to rise, but her hands were grabbed on both sides. Her face was held in the blood. She suddenly realized what was happening. Someone, some others were meaning to drown her, drown her in beauty-giving blood.

But that couldn't be.

She was the mistress of the manor. She owned everything. Who was doing this to her?

Anger flared inside. She struggled, but the others were too strong. The realization that she was going to die raced through her mind.

No.

They couldn't kill her.

Not now.

Not when she had achieved such beauty.

Darkness clouded her brain, as air burst from her lungs. She knew she would be soon be dead.

With her dying power, she cursed any and all for the perfidy she endured.   Revenge would be the sole project of her eternity.

READ THE REST

HERE ARE SOME OF MY OTHER BOOKS

Ghosts and Haunted Houses: a British Hauntings Collection Sixteen books– http://a-fwd.to/58aWoW8

The British Hauntings Series

The Haunting of Elleric Lodge - http://a-fwd.to/6aa9u0N

The Haunting of Fairview House - http://a-fwd.to/6lKwbG1

The Haunting of Weaver House - http://a-fwd.to/7Do5KDi

The Haunting of Grayson House - http://a-fwd.to/3nu8fqk

The Haunting of Keira O'Connell - http://a-fwd.to/2qrTERv

The Haunting of Ferncoombe Manor

http://a-fwd.to/32MzXfz

The Haunting of Highcliff Hall - http://a-fwd.to/2Fsd7F6

The Haunting of Harrow House - http://a-fwd.to/aQkzLPf

The Haunting of Stone Street Cemetery

http://a-fwd.to/1txL6vk

The Haunting of Rochford House http://a-fwd.to/6hbXYp0

The Haunting of Knoll House http://a-fwd.to/1GC9MrD

The Haunting of the Grey Lady http://a-fwd.to/4EUSjb7

The Haunting of Blakely Manor http://a-fwd.to/3b2B631

The Yuletide Haunting http://a-fwd.to/7a5QF4S

The Haunting of Fort Recluse http://a-fwd.to/3Hz77IX

The Haunting Trap http://a-fwd.to/5hw7zJ8

The Haunting of Montgomery House http://a-fwd.to/20ia6sP

The Haunting of Mackenzie Keep http://a-fwd.to/7n2AWxp

The Haunting of Gatesworld Manor http://a-fwd.to/3XlZUEK

The Haunting of The Lost Traveller Tavern http://a-fwd.to/3GAG1nG

The Haunting of the House on the Hill http://a-fwd.to/1X2Wtcn

The Haunting of Hemlock Grove Manor http://a-fwd.to/LpE0k9j

The Haunting of St. Lucian Peak
https://geni.us/LucianPeak

Christmas Ghosts and Haunted Houses
https://geni.us/PTLR0

The Haunting of Coven Castle
https://geni.us/CovenCastle

The Haunting of Creeping Fog Manor
https://geni.us/CreepingFog

The Haunting of Lost Souls House
https://geni.us/LostSoulsHouse

The Ghost Sight Chronicles

The Haunting on the Ridgeway - http://a-fwd.to/1bGBJ6O

Cursed to Haunt - http://a-fwd.to/7BiHzLj

The Revenge Haunting. http://a-fwd.to/67V0NBO

About the Author

Cat Knight has been fascinated by fantasy and the paranormal since she was a child. Where others saw animals in clouds, Cat saw giants and spirits. A mossy rock was home to faeries, and laying beneath the earth another dimension existed.

That was during the day.

By night there were evil spirits lurking in the closet and under her bed. They whirled around her in the witching hour, daring her to come out from under her blanket and face them. She breathed in a whisper and never poked her head out from under her covers nor got up in the dark no matter how scared she was, because for sure, she would die at the hands of ghosts or demons.

How she ever grew up without suffocating remains a mystery.

RECEIVE THE HAUNTING OF LILAC HOUSE FREE!

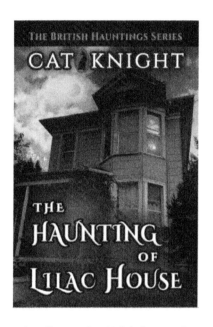

When you subscribe to Cat Knight's newsletter for new release announcements

SUBSCRIBE HERE

Like me on Facebook

.

Printed in Great Britain
by Amazon

40245462R00066